Praise for Banana Yoshimoto's

N.P.

"Yoshimoto throws four trendy young Japanese into a quandary that involves the reader instantly. Swept up by her heroine, Kazami Kano, off we run through the streets of Tokyo. . . . Almost one with the girl, we feel the oppressive summer heat, her loneliness, blind trust and choking fear. . . ."

—Nancy W. Olson, *Milwaukee Journal*

"Yoshimoto's writing is so wonderfully descriptive. . . . Readers—even those past their twenties—are likely to feel drawn in."

—Georgea Kovanis, *Detroit Free Press*

"Yoshimoto has given readers a snapshot of a generation of Japanese women caught between traditional expectations that define them in male-dominated marriages and their desire to remain young, pure and free."

—Robert Johnson, *Denver Post*

"Japan's leading pop novelist follows her successful debut with an ambitious novel of darker themes—incest, suicide, and the supernatural—that recalls more classic Japanese fiction. . . . A contemporary, hip treatment of a potentially lurid plot makes for a read that nonetheless resonates with echoes of the past. Offbeat but sound."

—*Kirkus Reviews*

"Compelling and clever. Yoshimoto writes with the sort of lucidity that usually takes hours and hours to appear so effortless. . . . But what really makes *N.P.* click . . . are the indomitable personalities of the main figures."

—David Finkle, *Trenton* (NJ) *Times*

"Charming. . . . Banana Yoshimoto has a way of writing about suicide and insomnia that's positively exuberant. . . . The narrators of her novels exude pure optimism, even as they suffer."

—Nathalie op de Beeck, *Washington City Paper*

Books by Banana Yoshimoto

Kitchen
N.P.

Published by WASHINGTON SQUARE PRESS

N.P.

A Novel by

BANANA YOSHIMOTO

Translated from the Japanese by Ann Sherif

WASHINGTON SQUARE PRESS
PUBLISHED BY POCKET BOOKS
New York   London   Toronto   Sydney   Tokyo   Singapore

This book is a work of fiction. Names, characters, places and incidents are products of the author's imagination or are used fictitiously. Any resemblance to actual events or locales or persons, living or dead, is entirely coincidental.

WSP

A Washington Square Press Publication of
POCKET BOOKS, a division of Simon & Schuster Inc.
1230 Avenue of the Americas, New York, NY 10020

Copyright © 1990 by Banana Yoshimoto. English translation rights arranged with Kadokawa Shoten Publishing Co., Ltd., through the Japan Foreign-Rights Centre.

Translation copyright © 1994 by Ann Sherif

Published by arrangement with Grove Press

ISBN: 0-671-89826-4

First Washington Square Press trade paperback printing March 1995

10 9 8 7 6 5 4 3 2 1

WASHINGTON SQUARE PRESS and colophon are registered trademarks of Simon & Schuster Inc.

Cover design by Rick Pracher
Cover photos by © Sigrid Estrada

Printed in the U.S.A.

N.P.

What did I know about Sarao Takase? I knew that he was an unhappy Japanese writer who had lived in the States, who had written some fiction when he wasn't in a blue funk. I knew that he had taken his own life at the age of forty-eight; that he and his estranged wife had had two children; and that his short stories had been published in a single volume and enjoyed several months of popularity in America.

The book contained ninety-seven stories and was called *N.P.* All of them are rather brief and discursive, like sketches. Takase did not have the perseverance to sustain an extended narrative. I found out about him from my old boyfriend, Shoji. He had discovered a ninety-eighth story by Takase, and was translating it.

You know how they say that if you're sitting around a bonfire on a hot summer night, telling one ghost story after another, something mysterious is bound to happen once you've reached the one-hundredth. Well, last summer, that happened to me. I lived through one of those one-hundredth stories, and it was precisely during the time of year when the air is intense and hot, and the blue summer sky promises to suck you up. Let me tell you the story that happened to me last summer.

I met Sarao Takase's children more than five years ago, when I was still in high school. One day, Shoji took me to a party hosted by a publisher. It was held in a large reception hall complete with miniature chandeliers decorated with orchids and huge tables laden with silver platters of fancy food. The room buzzed with people chatting and sampling the hors d'oeuvres. I looked around for other people my age, but I didn't see any at first. Then, I caught sight of Takase's kids, and I felt more at ease.

At one point, when Shoji was talking to someone else, I took the opportunity to move to a spot where I could see them better. It was really weird. I was overwhelmed by the sensation that I had actually met them before in my dreams, but then, in the next moment, I came back to my senses, aware that anyone who saw these two would feel the same way. They were, in some sense, a couple who evoked nostalgia, a longing for home.

Shoji caught me staring at them, and said, "Those two are the last living traces of Sarao Takase."

"They're both his children?" I asked.

"Yes, fraternal twins."

"I'd like to meet them."

"I'll introduce you."

"Just remember that I'm supposed to be twenty and a newcomer, okay?" I smiled.

"That sounds respectable enough. I'll take you over." He smiled too.

"Just a minute. I want to watch them a little longer."

I wanted to linger in the perfect spot that I had found for spying on them. Once introduced, I wouldn't be able to observe them so carefully. All I knew was that they were born when their parents were very young and still newlyweds, and that they were about my age. I had heard that their father had left the family when they were children, and that they had returned to Japan with their mother in order to be close to the Takase family. What a life.

I couldn't keep my eyes off them. Both were tall, with brownish hair. The girl was slender but healthy, and her skin glowed. She had an innocent face, but wore a tight, calf-length dress that was cut low in the back. She looked sexy; she looked perky—what can I say?

The guy was really sharp, too. He looked extremely robust, the picture of a vital, hopeful young man—except for those dark eyes. There was a glint of craziness in those eyes, which made me wonder about what he might have inherited from his father.

For some reason, they were always smiling. They just stood there talking, and laughing and smiling at one another. As I gazed at them, I realized that I had witnessed something like this before.

One day a long time before, I took a walk over to the botanical garden not far from home. Inside, I saw a mother stretched out on the broad lawn, a baby in her arms. The warm rays of the setting sun bathed the grass in a brilliant yellow green, and no one else was around. The young mother lay the child down on a white towel. She didn't play with the baby or talk to it, but instead just sat there gazing at it. Now and again, she looked up at the sky, deep in thought.

Her hair blew gently in the breeze, glowing in the sunlight. It was a still scene, not unlike a Wyeth painting, with intensely dark shadows against the light. I saw it as an omniscient narrator would, a portrait of an eternal sunset in which happiness and sadness became one.

Something similar happened when I was looking at the Takases. The melancholy of a brilliant evening sky. Perhaps that was an indication of the talent that flowed in their veins, something that neither youth nor idle pleasures could suppress.

I asked Shoji, "Have you decided to translate Sarao Takase's stories?"

"That's my plan," he said proudly.

"What's the book called, anyway? Some initials or something?"

"N.P."

"What does that stand for?"

"North Point."

"North Point? I don't get it."

"It's the title of an old song."

"What kind of song?"

"A very sad one," he replied.

That day, the phone shook me from a deep sleep. Still in bed, I groped for the receiver.

"Hi, Kazami. It's me. How're you doing?"

I heard my older sister's low voice float out of the receiver. The choppy sound you always get on international calls brought me to my senses.

"What's wrong?"

"Oh, everything's fine. I just wanted to hear your voice," my sister said.

"You forgot the time difference again! It's five o'clock in the morning here," I said.

"Sorry."

"What time is it there?"

"Eight at night."

This time difference thing made me feel really strange. I was thankful for that telephone line, the only thing that connected me to my sister.

"How are you?" I asked.

"I just wanted you to know that I dreamed about you the

other night," my sister said. "In the dream, I saw you walking through the neighborhood, holding hands with an older man."

"What neighborhood? Your neighborhood in London?"

"Right. Back there behind the church."

"Wow. Sounds good to me," I said happily. I knew that my sister's dreams did, in fact, often come true.

"Yeah, but you know, you both looked sad, and I couldn't talk to you. The guy was tall and kind of high-strung looking, and had on a white sweater. You were wearing your student uniform. So I thought that maybe you were having an affair with some older guy just to make a point."

"No way." A chill ran down my spine, even as the words came out of my mouth. That had to have been me walking with Shoji in her dream. But my sister never knew about Shoji.

"Oh no, I've lost my touch," she said.

"Don't worry. It happens to the best of us."

But my mind was working furiously. Was this an omen? It was true—he had been on my mind a lot then, but not because I was trying to remember him. His image would appear to me out of nowhere in a cloudy sky, on a wet, black asphalt street, on a shop window, even though he had been absent from my conscious memory.

"How's your husband?"

"Oh, he's fine. We're coming to Japan in the winter. How's Mom? Do you see her often?"

"Yeah, every so often. She misses you a lot."

"Tell her hi for me, okay? Sorry I woke you up. I'll call again soon."

"Try figuring out the time difference before you do, okay?"

"Consider it done. Anyway, you stay away from bad love affairs, hear me?" She laughed.

I reassured her that I would, and we said good-bye. After I hung up, the quiet of the room took shape and pressed in on me. The room was soon full of the pale blue of early dawn.

I had to go and check on them. I stumbled out of bed and found my way to my desk. Inside the bottom cabinet door was a box that I had hardly ever opened. It contained a worn paperback copy of *N.P.*, a notebook, and a heavy Rolex watch. These were my mementos of Shoji.

Four years earlier, he had killed himself with an overdose of sleeping pills. From the moment that these objects came into my possession, I have regarded them as my treasures, my heart and soul. Sometimes when I'm working at the university, and I hear the distant sound of sirens screaming through the city, I wonder if the fire might be somewhere near my house, and if Shoji's things are safe. They mean that much to me.

I took each of these objects in my hands to make sure they were intact, and then carefully stored them away in the box. Only then could I rest peacefully.

Until I was nineteen, I lived with my mother and sister. My parents got divorced when I was nine and my sister eleven. They split up when my father fell in love with another woman. Up until then, my mother had a busy career as a freelance interpreter, but after the divorce, she decided to do translations at home so she could be there for us kids. She accepted any work that came her way, from ghost translations to interviews.

We missed having a father around, but we had a good time together anyway. Strictly speaking my family consisted of a mother and two daughters, but our ages and roles changed many times each day. I might be the one who comforted Mother when she was in tears, and she would encourage me when I was moaning and groaning about my problems—or it might be my sister who took that motherly role. In times of need, someone was always there to give you a hug. All of us were willing to straighten out misunderstandings and anger. And we got used to living that way.

At one point, Mother decided that she wanted to spend more time with us, and so she started teaching us English. Every night about ten o'clock, we'd sit down at the kitchen table with our notebooks and study for an hour—English pronunciation, vocabulary, simple phrases, that kind of thing. I was just a kid, and was not thrilled at the idea of daily English lessons, but I went along with it for Mother's sake.

So when I think of my mother, I don't think of a figure bent over the kitchen sink, but rather of a plain face with wire-rimmed glasses sitting next to me during English lessons. I recall her pale fingers flipping through her thick dictionaries at an amazing speed while she worked on translations. As she taught us, she was retracing the lines of her own life back to the beginning, chiseling onto her own mind that basic—no, rudimentary—English one more time.

I don't live with Mother anymore, but every time I see her, she happily reminds me that her English lessons were the reason I was able to get work as a research assistant for an English professor and the reason my sister married a foreigner. It's because I taught the two of you how much fun English could be, she tells me. That's what I love best about my mother.

The next morning, I woke up with a start. The first thing that entered my vision was a clear blue summer sky, shining through an opening in the curtains. It was very similar in tone to a dream I had been having recently. In the dream, I was crying. It felt like I had brought home some gold dust from the pristine river in my dream.

I wondered whether I was crying because I was sad, or because I had just been released from my sadness. Either way, I didn't want to wake up yet. A cool breeze blew in from the window that I had left open a crack the night before.

Even after I got to work that day, I couldn't shake the feeling. To make matters worse, I kept making mistakes. It was one thing after another. First I broke a teacup, and then I messed up on the Xerox machine. Something was wrong. I felt weird, like the sensations from that dream had intruded on reality. Then I realized that my mind had been totally occupied with trying to figure out what exactly it was that I had dreamt.

That's why I failed to answer that phone call, and just let it ring and ring. It was at least my tenth mistake of the morning. My boss finally picked up the receiver and glared at me as he said hello. That brought me back to my senses.

"Kano. It's for you."

With a look of consternation, he handed me the phone. I apologized and put the receiver up to my ear, but there was nothing. Whoever it was had hung up.

"Did they give a name?" I asked him, puzzled.

"No, just asked for you. It was a woman. Hey, why don't you take your lunch now? You seem tired today."

"But it's only eleven o'clock." Everyone in the office had been pretending not to notice my ineptness that morning, but when I objected to the professor's offer of an early lunch, they all urged me to go. On their insistence, I left the office.

I walked across the playing field to the edge of the campus, wondering all the while if I were really acting that weird. I didn't feel so strange. It was just that my body hadn't gotten used to reality yet, and the world appeared fresh and new.

Perhaps it had been a dream about being born—maybe that was it.

There was a bookstore up on the hill back behind the campus. I climbed the slope toward the shop, hoping to find something there to read during my long two-hour lunch. There, in the middle of the street, I ran into Otohiko. It was only our second encounter. It was somewhere just past where the road I was on (the one that runs up the hill) intersects with a busy street lined with shops. I had idly glanced down that street and caught sight of the neon pink and silver plastic cherry-blossom streamers that hung from the telephone poles, fluttering brightly against the blue sky. Even now I can see the vivid after-image of those colors dancing before my eyes. When I looked back up the hill, I noticed someone walking down the slope toward me. It was a man whom I had seen before.

"I know you." The words slipped out of my mouth. "You're Sarao Takase's son."

"Excuse me?" he said with a suspicious glance. It was only natural that he would be wary. I lost no time in introducing myself.

"We met once a long time ago at a publisher's party. My name is Kazami Kano."

He studied my face carefully and then nodded. "You were with Shoji Toda, the translator, weren't you?"

"You have a good memory."

"Yeah, well, you were practically the only other person under thirty at the party," he said with a grin.

"Do you live around here?" I asked.

"My family's house is in Yokohama, but I'm staying at my sister's now. She lives up at the top of this hill, and she's in graduate school at T. University."

"At T.U.?"

"Yeah."

"What a coincidence. I work in the English department there."

"Oh yeah? You've already met my sister. She was at the party with me that night. Her name is Saki."

"Then I've probably seen her on campus without realizing who she was."

"Are you free now? Want to go for some coffee?"

I had nothing but time.

"Sure."

The lunch crowd hadn't appeared yet, so the café was practically empty. We found a table and ordered some coffee. To me, Otohiko existed only in the past, in an old story, and I had never imagined that I would see him again. Now that I had him here before me, I saw that something had happened to him. Those extraordinarily dark eyes seemed out of place with his casual polo shirt and glowing cheeks. I hadn't felt that way when I first met him.

"You've changed a lot, Otohiko."

"Do you think so?"

"You're only two years older than me, but you look so mature. See, I know how old you are and everything."

"So you're twenty-two?"

"Right."

"So you were still in high school when I saw you at that party."

"Uh-huh."

"That was five years ago. Unbelievable. I thought that I hadn't aged a bit, but that shows what I know. But then I've been abroad."

"Where?"

"Boston. I just got back to Japan in April."

It wasn't only Otohiko's appearance that had changed. He had become closed and cautious, somehow, as it is so often with people who have desperately sought to preserve their pride, even as some cruel, twisted fate pursues them.

"Before you went to Boston, you lived in Japan for a long time?"

"Yeah, with my grandparents in Yokohama."

"You came back right after your father died?"

"Right. My father left us when I was little, but our names were still on his family register. My grandparents wanted their grandchildren around, so they asked us to come live with them."

"How old were you then?"

"Fourteen or so. My sister and I realized how messed up Mom was getting after our father died, and so we played the adults and invited her to go on a trip with us. We traveled all over the place, but when the trip was over and it was time to go home, we didn't know what to do next. That was when my grandparents called and said that we should come live with them in Yokohama. Mom felt strange about accepting their offer, but my sister and I insisted that we go. We knew it would be best for her in the long run. My grandparents wouldn't have stood in the way if she had wanted to remarry, and she might have lost it if just the three of us continued living together. Of course, we didn't want to leave the States—that was our home—but we put up a brave front and took the plunge."

"I know what you're talking about. My family was the same way. After my parents got divorced, it was just me and my sister and our mother."

"You know it's not healthy living in a family like that."

"You said it. The absent party takes on this enormous presence. My father wasn't there, but life revolved around him, anyway."

"Right, and sometimes everyone gets really neurotic."

"Absolutely," I agreed. "You know what happened to me? I literally couldn't talk for a while."

"Because of the way your family was?" he asked curiously.

"I guess so. I lost my voice for no apparent reason and then it returned just as mysteriously."

"So there was some kind of terrible struggle going on inside that little girl's body then."

Three months after my father left us, I lost my voice in a vain attempt to keep Mother from falling apart. I can't tell you how tense she was then. The day it happened, I had been playing outside in the snow for a long time after school, and by evening I came down with a fever. For a couple of days, I stayed home in bed. My whole body ached, and my throat was sore and swollen.

One day, while I was lying there in bed on my side, delirious with fever, I could hear my mother and sister's voices.

"How do you know?" my mother was saying.

"Well, it's just a hunch, but I feel pretty certain about it," my sister replied.

"You mean that Kazami is going to lose her voice entirely?" Mother asked, in that hysterical tone that we heard so often in those days.

"Yeah, I think so," my sister said blithely.

My sister did have good intuition, and could usually tell you who was on the other end when the phone rang, or when the weather was going to change, or just any little thing. She would always announce her predictions in a strangely calm manner, and was very mature about it all.

I heard Mother say, in a rather shaky voice, "You mustn't tell Kazami about this now."

"Sure," my sister said.

I was curiously unfazed by the thought that I might lose my voice but, just to test out her theory, I tried to squeeze out a voice from my parched throat. All that emerged was scratchy noise. I raised my head so that I could see over the ice pack. Outside the window, a block of clouds, dyed a brilliant pink by the rays of the setting sun, extended far into the western sky. For a brief moment in my delirium, I couldn't tell just what was real. Had Father really left us, and started another family? And Mother's nightly English lessons, and the pure, deep white snow that covered the playground at school, and the fuzzy halos around the street lights as I walked home, feverish, on that day. It was too much.

Just as she had predicted, my voice didn't return, even after the flu was gone. Both Mother and my sister couldn't be comforted, and the doctor naturally hinted that it might be psychosomatic. On the way home from the doctor's office, tears kept welling up in Mother's eyes. Without question, we were all nervous, and terrified of losing control of our own bodies.

At first I felt like a wreck over having lost my voice, but my spirits improved when Mother relaxed a bit herself and told me that I should just take it easy. Instead of going to school during the day, I stayed home. I left the house only early in the morning and after dark.

A person without a voice gradually loses language. For the first two days, my thought processes remained the same as before. If my sister stepped on my foot, I would think "ouch" in words. When a place I had been to before appeared on TV, my thoughts would virtually be in the same form as the words that might have come out of my mouth at that moment, had I been able to speak—like, "Oh, I know where that is. I wonder when they filmed this," or something like that.

19

But after a period of being unable to speak those words, something changed in my head. I came to see the array of colors that lay behind words. When my sister was being nice to me, I perceived a brilliant image of pink light. My mother's words and gestures when she was teaching us English were gold; a bright yellow orange came through the palm of my hand when I bent down to pat our cat as she wandered by.

Living like that utterly convinced me of the extreme limitations of language. I was just a child then, so I had only an intuitive understanding of the degree to which one loses control of words once they are spoken or written. It was then that I first felt a deep curiosity about language, and understood it as a tool that encompasses both a single moment and eternity.

It came back just as suddenly. One rainy afternoon, my sister and I were sitting together at the dining-room table waiting for Mom to come home. I was sitting there in a daze, not quite asleep, watching my sister read her magazine. She turned the pages one after another, with the regularity and rhythm of dripping water. The neighbor's TV blended in with the sound of the rain. The windows of the room were steamed up, and the room felt very warm.

And I started thinking about how Mother would come home soon, grocery bags in both hands. She would look a little tired, but go straight to the kitchen and set to work making our dinner. The miso soup left over from breakfast, some fish or chicken from the supermarket deli, her special salad, and fruit. I could nearly smell the rice cooking. Presently, she would bring dinner in to us. After we ate, we'd have our English lessons, watch TV, take a bath, and she'd tuck us into bed. I could hear her slippered feet pad into the next room as I drifted off to sleep.

It was a warm, happy home. It felt secure, as if we had a big family, even though there were only the three of us.

And then my sister said to me, "Are you asleep, Kazami?"

"Mm-huh," I answered.

I had tried to talk and it worked. It sounded really strange because my voice seemed like it came from far away. A welcome sound it was.

"Kazami, did you say something just now?" my sister asked in shock.

"I guess so," I replied gingerly.

"So have you been able to talk all this time?"

"No, I really couldn't talk."

"What did it feel like? Was it hard?"

"No. I felt like I was finally understanding some things."

I recall that we kept talking and talking, just to make sure that my voice had actually returned.

★　★　★

I said to Otohiko, "When I got my voice back, it was as if the whole family had survived some kind of endless night. I mean, we didn't realize it then, but in retrospect."

"Yeah, it sounds like what happened in my family. I refused to go to school. I pretended that I was going, but I actually went to a part-time job instead. I lied about my age so I could get work," he explained. "Finally, they found out what I was up to and I caught hell. That was the first time I really felt close to my grandparents."

"Oh yeah?" I said. "This is so strange. I feel like I'm sitting with a character from a story."

"Who, me?"

"Like meeting a character I've only read about in real life."

He laughed. After a moment's hesitation, he said, "Shoji killed himself, didn't he?"

"Yeah. Right when he was translating *N.P.*"

"You two were still together then?"

"Yes."

"Wow."

"But he didn't do it because you two gave him the ninety-eighth story, you know."

"He told you that we did that?" Otohiko's eyes widened.

"Yeah, he said the manuscript had come from Takase's survivors. He told me that he was going to translate that story too and have the whole thing published in Japan."

"What a shame," he said. It seemed like he was hiding something, but it wasn't as if Shoji would come back to life if I found out his secret. I didn't pursue it any further.

"Publishers just aren't interested in it anymore." I smiled. "The book is cursed."

"It's gotta be. The three people who attempted to translate it into Japanese are all dead. You knew about that?"

"I did. The college professor who started it first, and the student who was assisting him, and then Shoji, right? And all suicides. How come?"

"It probably has to do with the process of putting his English into Japanese. As a matter of fact, Saki has been investigating that very question. I wish that everyone would just forget about that book, and the people involved as well. It was no coincidence that they ended up dead. Everyone who is attracted to this book, everyone who wants to translate it, they all have a death wish. The book calls them."

"That's a scary way of looking at it," I said.

"Why? Do you like the book?" he asked.

"Yes, I found it quite fascinating."

I had read it many times. When I'm reading it, I always get this feeling of a thick, hot liquid brewing in my heart. A new universe enters my body, and takes on a life of its own within me. Not long after Shoji died, I tried translating some of *N.P.*, too. Whether because of the book itself or the difficulty of that time in my life, I was terrified. A black vapor would fill my lungs whenever I was translating that English into Japanese. I simply couldn't get the feeling out of my head. It felt like walking out into the ocean with your clothes on, the waves pounding into your body, and swimming out toward the horizon, with nothing holding you back. Like that sensation of wet clothes clinging to your body. Fortunately, I was still a young high school student then so I gave up translating the book. Quitting was a sign of a healthy mind—I think.

What would be an appropriate metaphor to explain my feelings when I was doing the translation? An endless meadow of golden pampas grass swaying in the wind, or a coral reef beneath a deep, brilliant blue ocean. That utter stillness you feel when you're seeing a whole bunch of tropical fish swimming by, all in bright colors, and they don't even look like living creatures.

You're not going to live long with that kind of world in your head. I looked at Otohiko and thought of the sadness that his father must have embraced.

"Japanese is a strange language. It really is. This might contradict what I said before, but I feel as if I've lived a very long time since I came to Japan. Even the language affects how you think. It wasn't until I started living here that I understood that my father was indeed Japanese and that, even when he wrote in English, Japanese was his true foundation. That's why such disastrous things happen when someone tries to translate his English into Japanese. Father's strong sense of longing for his homeland is such an integral part of the text. He should have written it in Japanese to begin with."

I felt the same way about a lot of what he said, although, to tell the truth, his explanation seemed somewhat garbled.

"Do you want to be a novelist?" I asked.

"I used to, but not anymore," he said.

"What do you think of the ninety-eighth story?"

Otohiko look puzzled. "In what sense?"

"You know, it's about incest, and I was wondering if your father was actually in love with your sister?"

Without hesitation, Otohiko said, "Definitely. I mean, I wasn't around him that much, but I do know that the guy was crazy."

That, indeed, was the subject of the ninety-eighth story. The main character gets divorced and starts leading this wild singles life. Then he falls in love with a teenage girl whom he met in a bar on the outskirts of town. Only after he has slept with her several times does he discover that she is his own daughter. By then, he's already become a captive of her bewitching charm.

"There's an element of *Lolita* in it, for sure, but that's not all. Like the end is really magical, maybe because of all the drugs and liquor they're doing. I especially liked the descriptions of the daughter's inhuman beauty. It reminded me of that Doyle painting of the mermaid," I said.

Otohiko blushed a little, but he nodded happily at my praise of his father. So he was proud after all.

"I wanted people in Japan to read that one."

"I think Saki—my sister—will translate it someday. She's been wanting to do it," he said. "Kazami, do you have the manuscript of the ninety-eighth story?"

"Yes, they gave it to me as something to remember Shoji by."

"Watch out, because there's someone who's after that manuscript."

"Who? Your sister?" I asked with surprise. Why did I need to be careful?

"No, not her. She would come and ask permission to make a copy of the manuscript if she wanted it. It's a woman who's really obsessed with the book. She's got a copy of the ninety-eighth story already, but she wants to have all the other existing copies."

"A friend of yours?"

"We were traveling together until recently. She came back

to Japan with me from the States. She seems to know all about you."

I smiled. "You were hanging out with a stalker?"

He smiled too. "Yeah, I'm into people who abandon themselves to passion."

"She must be in love with Takase's son, too."

"Yeah, I like that twist to the story myself."

"You're a strange one too, Otohiko."

"I feel like I've known you for a long time. It's weird."

"We *have* known each other for a long time."

"It's true. Since we've both spent a long time thinking about that book, we have many things in common. It's so easy to talk with you."

"I still think about it sometimes," I said.

"Oh, me too. Probably just about every day. It's part of me physically, kind of like a curse," Otohiko muttered in a low voice. I was struck by those words.

We agreed to meet again soon, and exchanged addresses before parting.

I still think about him sometimes. About Shoji, that is. I was in high school when I fell in love with him. We were crazy, wild in love with each other, totally enraptured. Even now, I can remember being with him almost every day, just hanging around his apartment, or sometimes helping him with the translation. For sure, Shoji seemed happy when he was with me. That was the absolute truth.

But I could do little to lessen the fatigue that had been building up in him before we even met, the weariness over the complications of his life. I was incapable of truly understanding the darkness that made up a large part of his personality, the blackness that I found so attractive. From the moment we met, I was a butterfly that flew into that space that was his soul, a room where the light had begun to dim. Although he may have regarded me as a welcome distraction, in fact, my presence only confused him more because I introduced flashes of daylight into his darkness.

So when I dream of Shoji now, the premise is always that the present me is with Shoji. This is merely wishful thinking on my part: if only the grown-up me could meet him, I could bring joy and calm into his life, rather than the dazzle of a teenage girl. Who knows, maybe it would be futile, but I still have such regrets. If I could only meet him again. This was my only hope. But maybe I'm overrating my own abilities.

But I nearly lose my mind when I hear others say that people who commit suicide can't go to heaven, and that they are permanently stuck in a state of misery. Before I can even object to such absurd statements, the image of his gentle smiling face flashes before my eyes. That smile that shut me out, that shut everyone out.

I was at Shoji's place the morning of the day he died. It was a dream I saw in the summer sunlight that poured in through the open curtains, one beautiful early summer morning, just like today.

Usually, Shoji got up before me. I needed to get to school so I'd drag myself out of bed around eight o'clock. By that time, Shoji would already be sitting at his computer, typing away. I liked the click of his fingers at the keyboard, and his attitude of concentration, because they brought back childhood memories of my mother.

Shoji was seventeen years older than me, and his tranquillity had the effect of calming my overflowing adolescent energy. When we were together, it was so quiet. We could be laughing or horsing around, but somehow it still felt calm. Like, even if I slept in and he knew that I was going to be late for school, he wouldn't wake me up. And then if I just decided to skip school, Shoji didn't chase me out of his apartment. That's the kind of guy he was.

That morning was different. After the alarm clock woke me up, I looked over and saw Shoji asleep beside me, his face pale and still. There were dark circles under his eyes, and his breathing was shallow. I was only eighteen, and seeing Shoji like that wrenched my heart. I gently pulled the blanket up over him, and got out of bed. I put on my school uniform, and had a glass of milk. Something seemed different in the air of that room on that most quiet morning.

And then I couldn't find my wristwatch. After a brief search, I gave up and decided to borrow one of Shoji's that I found on his desk. It felt like ten pounds on my wrist, and the glass covering the black face glittered like ice. I felt so depressed, almost homesick, standing there all alone in an apartment that wasn't my own.

You know, that morning, everything stood so still—in the apartment and outdoors—so quiet that I could practically hear Shoji's breathing from where I stood across the room. I moved stiffly and awkwardly around the place, and it felt suffocating. The hard copy of his translation of the ninety-eighth story lay on his computer desk. I picked it up, and noticed that only half of the story was there. That surprised me, because Shoji had just told me that he had finished translating the whole thing. Then, the day before, he had been very depressed, and said that he just couldn't get the translation right. As I stood there at his desk, I realized that he had started it all over again, from the beginning. I remembered the other two translators who had killed themselves, and a chill ran down my spine.

On the pad of paper on his desk, I wrote a note for him:

As soon as you're done with the translation, let's go to the beach, just like we did a couple of weeks ago. We can go early, change into our suits there, and sunbathe on the sand. We can just talk, about everything. It'll be fun. Oh, and I borrowed your watch. I'll bring it back soon.

I hoped that the smell of the ocean and the sound of the waves would come into his mind when he read my note. Maybe he would get in the mood for the beach, and get his work done so we could be together. It wasn't jealousy I felt so much as fear. I wrote the note in defiance of the hidden darkness that was my enemy.

I wanted him to remember all the things we had seen

31

together when we had just fallen in love: the wet warmth of our nocturnal embraces; the beauty of the orange sunlight on the buildings at dawn, when he would walk me down to the street and put me, sleepy, into a taxi; tears; the warmth of our palms pressed together; the heady scents of those days. I searched my mind desperately, like a woman about to be abandoned by her lover in the last stages of a love affair.

I felt worried about him, and so I called him from a public phone near school at lunchtime.

"Hello." His voice sounded just fine.

"I'm calling from school," I said with relief. I knew that he could hear the screaming and shouting from the kids fooling around in the school yard, and the students splashing around as they cleaned the swimming pool. I laughed and said, "Pretty noisy, huh?"

"Amazing," Shoji replied. "Have you eaten lunch yet?"

"Well, I had to eat a school lunch because I wasn't at home last night."

He laughed. "You really are just a high school student, aren't you?" He sounded envious. "Thanks for your note."

"I'll come over in a couple days."

"Okay."

The school yard behind me overflowed with the clamor and laughter of students. They seemed so happy and full of life to me, like they were reveling in the thirty-minute lunch break, their only free time of the whole day. Their voices filled the air, and their energy exploded all around me. I looked up and saw the dazzling blue summer sky. On that brilliant afternoon, light and shadow raced across the street.

"Talk to you later."

"Bye."

We hung up. That was the last time we spoke. How far apart we were then, each on our own end of the telephone line, farther apart than heaven and hell, and so complicated. I didn't say how much I loved him. I didn't even try to, nor did any means exist for communicating or receiving that message, or for knowing it.

I had heard people say that things like this happen between people in love, but I myself didn't know that such emptiness really existed. I wanted to believe that these were stories set in another world, long, long ago, in tales of failed love set in a barren desert. It could never happen now. I had my own utopia.

It was two or three days after I had coffee with Otohiko. That afternoon, I was packing my stuff and getting ready to leave the office, when I heard someone call loudly from the doorway.

"Is Ms. Kano here?"

"Yes, may I help you?" I went out to see who it was, and discovered a young woman standing there. She looked nice. Then I remembered what he had told me.

"I'm Saki Takase." She introduced herself with a smile. "I was so surprised when my brother told me that you worked here, too."

Compared to her brother, Saki looked much more together than she had when I saw her at the party. She was wearing a really sharp outfit, and her smiling face looked like a flower. I remember having a similar impression when I met her at the party, but now she emanated an even greater femininity.

"I was going to say that it was nice to meet you again, but we didn't really get to talk at that party, did we?" I said.

"That's true, but I remember you well anyway. I'm happy to see you again. Are you on your way out? Would you like to have dinner together? If you're not busy, that is," Saki said.

I nodded. "Yes, I'd like to. It would be nice to talk."

She didn't say anything in response, but just smiled sweetly. That smile entranced me, and made my heart feel pure.

We left my office and walked across the campus toward a nearby French restaurant. It was that time of day when the hazy blue sky starts to inhale the heat of the day.

"The sky already looks like summer," Saki observed.

"Yeah. Do you have air-conditioning in the psych department? We don't have any, and it's like a broiler in the summer."

She smiled. "Of course we don't. That's why I'm always trying to find an excuse to work in the library."

Her name Saki meant blossom, and it suited her well. She overflowed with gentleness and light. She was wide eyed, as if she were looking forward to the future with hope.

* * *

The restaurant was packed with students. The rays of the setting sun flowed in through the plate-glass windows in front, dying the whole room a bright orange. We ordered soup and a baguette for me, a sandwich for Saki, and then crab salad and a carafe of white wine to share. There's no better way to get to know a person than having a meal together. Saki and I had hit it off well from the moment we met anyway, and at the restaurant we really relaxed and had a good talk.

"Do you live by yourself?" I asked.

"No, Otohiko has been staying with me since he got back from Boston. It's just too much of a commute from Yokohama. I always go home to our grandparents on the weekends, though, devoted granddaughter that I am. Mom and I go shopping and stuff. It's rough being an only daughter."

"It must be hard for your mom not having her kids close by."

"I don't know. I mean, normally a widow wouldn't go and live with her in-laws, especially if they were in a foreign country, but Mom is the type who stays at home all the time, and my grandparents are unbelievably kind to her, so they all get along. Pretty weird, huh?"

"Yeah, that's the part of your life story I always have a hard time with."

"My mother went through so much with my father that

now nothing fazes her. How about you, Kazami? Do you live alone?"

"Yes, we stopped living together as a family three years ago, when my sister got married to a British guy and moved to England. After that, we split up. My father is living by himself now, and my mom remarried two years ago. She and her husband live in Setagaya. So I've been on my own since college."

"Where's your place?"

"Oh, over in F."

"So you're close. I wonder why we've never run into each other before."

"I was wondering that myself."

"That was funny how you recognized Otohiko on the street."

"I might not have if he had been in a crowd of people. But there we were on that hill, with no one else around. It was fate."

"For some reason, both of us had clear memories of you, too. I can't figure it out. We never even talked with you at the party."

"Oh, it's probably because I was standing there staring at the two of you," I laughed.

"When I heard about Mr. Toda's death, the first person I thought of was you," she said.

I just nodded. "I didn't even go to the funeral. I just couldn't. Do you know what I mean?"

"Oh, yeah, it just blew you away, right?" Saki said.

"You're researching their suicides, I hear."

"Actually, I started out wanting to translate the book myself, but then I got scared, for a couple of reasons. There was my own father's death, and I'd heard about suicide running in families. Plus, all those other people translating it who chose death. At first, I thought maybe I could do a good job of it, what with my background and all. I decided I had to find out why they all did it, and then I got sidetracked and started studying psychology. Anyway, I have a lot of things that I want to accomplish," Saki said.

"I'd like to see the complete translation of that book out in Japanese. If you need any help with it, let me know. I helped Shoji with it some, and I'm still alive. I can handle it!" I said with a smile.

"If somebody heard us, they'd think we were talking about poison or explosives or something."

"Maybe that's how dangerous that book really is," I suggested, and Saki nodded in agreement.

★　★　★

As we were leaving the restaurant, I felt optimistic. The summer promised to be lots of fun. We emerged on the muggy street, and I said to Saki, "Let's have lunch or something together sometime soon."

And Saki said, "Yes, let's do. We have so much to talk about. I think this summer's going to be lots of fun."

She turned and smiled at me. What had just happened, mental telepathy? We waved good-bye, just like old friends, and parted.

As I walked away, I realized that Saki had barely mentioned her brother. Perhaps that's what happens when you grow up, but I felt a twinge of regret at the loss of the couple I had seen at the party that day, so compatible and close, always smiling.

I love making new friends like that. And it worked out perfectly with Saki. Summer had just begun, and then Saki appeared, so friendly and open, like someone I'd been friends with for a long time—plus she lived nearby. I had no special vacation plans, no steady boyfriend, and so I felt really excited about the prospects. Several things remained a mystery to me, though. The call from my sister. And Saki herself—I couldn't tell what kept her so strong. And then there was Otohiko, mumbling things about the ninety-eighth story, and living in a foreign country with some woman who's obsessed with his father the writer. That phone call for me at the office, with no one on the other end.

I didn't have doubts about them. I just knew that there must be more to the story. On the surface, it appeared that I had run into a couple of people I'd once known, and we would spend a pleasant summer together. It didn't feel that simple, though. What was it then? I would sit in a daze, doing my mental detective work. What was still hidden? I had no way of finding out then, but the ninety-eighth story kept popping into my mind. Intuitively, I knew that it had something to do with them.

In the story, the man falls apart after he has the affair with his own daughter. Her murmurs sound like the distant pounding of ocean waves, and her slender ankles, illuminated in the moonlight, remind him of a mermaid's tail. Was it Saki? I wondered, but had no way of knowing. I would have to wait to find out. Faced by this uncertainty, knowing only that something would happen, I prayed that I could rise to the challenge. Since Shoji's death, I had been thinking about life that way.

Since we spent so much of our time on the same campus, Saki and I ended up doing a lot of things together. Right before summer vacation, the campus suddenly bustled with students coming in for their exams. That day, the two of us were in the cafeteria.

"This place really feels like a campus at this time of year, don't you think?" Saki commented between sips of coffee.

"I'm just happy that it's other people who are taking the tests, and not me." I was having orange juice.

"Do you like summer?"

"I adore it. That's all I think about."

"It's true love then."

"How about you?" I asked Saki.

"Spring is my favorite. But I know what you mean about summer. I can tell how much you love it, just from the expression on your face."

"I absolutely crave summer. I can't wait." I smiled at Saki, and then, abruptly, asked, "What's up with Otohiko these days?"

"Why do you ask?"

"It's just that I haven't seen him since that day."

Saki shook her head. "He's always hanging out at her house."

"Oh, you mean that woman he was traveling with?" I said.

"Yeah, I'm completely fed up with him. I have no idea what will happen to them. She's worse than before they left for Boston together."

"Is she bad news?"

"Terrible. And she's gotten worse, too."

"He's completely sold on her, right?"

She had a strong grip on him. I felt a tinge of longing. I had really enjoyed talking with Otohiko.

"Oh, but his love life is really none of my business, is it? I'll tell you the whole story next time we have lunch, if you'd like."

"Whenever you feel like it. You done? I've got to get back."

We went out, and I felt so excited about all the signs of summer—the bright sunshine, the sparkling black asphalt, the deep, still green of a grove of trees. Saki saw me take a deep breath, and she smiled, her face like a big sunflower. "I bet all this really turns you on." I had to narrow my eyes a bit because her face looked so bright and lovely in the sunlight. Summer was almost here.

The arrival of summer promised me some time for relaxation, but, in fact, I ended up with daily requests from a lot of different people for assistance on translations. They all wanted me to prepare a preliminary translation, on the sly, for the preliminary translation that they were working on for a professor. All of the instructors were probably busy with the same kind of part-time summer jobs, as well. Sure, I earned some spending money, but every job had a tight deadline, and it ended up feeling like homework the teacher had assigned for summer vacation. So I showed up at school almost every day, and I stayed up late flipping through dictionaries.

One day, very late at night, rain was pouring outside like a typhoon. The rain beat down so hard and the wind so strong that I didn't even hear the approaching footsteps. When I heard the sudden knock on the door, I nearly jumped out of my skin. It was three o'clock in the morning. Trembling, I peeked out through the peephole in the front door. It was Otohiko. I decided to let him in.

"What are you doing here so late? A confession of love?" I asked.

"Something like that," he said.

He came stumbling in the door, very drunk, his umbrella drenched and his leather shoes soaking wet. My heart skipped a beat. It seemed so much like a soap opera.

"Something's happened with your girlfriend?" I asked.

"No, no, that's not it."

"You've been drinking?"

"I got into this argument that really bummed me out, and then I drank a lot. Now I don't even know if what I was saying was right or not. I had to consult with someone who would know. Sorry it's so late—the liquor made me do it."

"I'm the someone who would know, I take it?"

"Yes." Otohiko nodded.

"Who were you debating with anyway? Saki?"

"No."

"Well what could I possibly have to do with all this? I barely know you."

"That's a tough one."

"You could have called. Or waited until tomorrow," I insisted.

"Sorry," he said, and stared down at the ground. Because

I have been known to get crazy drunk like that myself, I knew that there was no malicious intent on his part. He just needed an answer. But what was the question?

"Okay, okay, come on in," I said.

Otohiko stood firm in the front hall. "No, I'm fine right here."

"This makes me nervous, standing out here. Come on in and sit down."

With that, he somehow managed to take off his shoes and step up out of the vestibule into the hall. Almost immediately, he said, "I have to use your bathroom. I feel like I'm going to throw up."

"You don't have to ask. Just go ahead."

He looked terrible. I hurriedly pushed him toward the bathroom.

It all happened so fast that I didn't even have time to feel disgusted. I heard him retch into the toilet and flush it down. I could do nothing but stand there by the bathroom door and wait for him. Finally he emerged and asked me for a glass of water. His face looked even paler than when he had first arrived, and his eyes were totally bloodshot.

"You look like you're about to die," I said as I passed the glass of water to him. He gulped it down.

"Do you remember that story?"

"Which one?"

"You know, that one about the man who gives you a lot of water as thanks for a favor, and you're in the desert, and then there's this big ladle, and some gold coins, I think." He muttered some nonsense.

"Oh, I get it. The water tasted good, right? You want some more?"

"Merci."

"Here, have a seat on the couch. You can lie down if you want."

I brought out another glass of water, and he gulped it down. The room grew quiet, and I suddenly realized how hard it was raining.

"I'm sorry," Otohiko said.

"Just relax. You can explain when you're ready. What did you want to ask me about?" I asked him, and sat down on the floor next to him.

"I'll tell you in a minute. Just give me a second."

"Is there something the matter?"

"You don't know the half of it," he said, and closed his eyes. The rain was falling even harder than before, and the windowpanes shook in the wind. The storm roared on, and I thought that it would never end.

"Don't fall asleep. You're scaring me."

I shook him by the shoulder.

"No, I'm not sleeping. I know. We'll make a copy of it right away. Just to be safe," he said.

"What are you talking about?"

"The ninety-eighth story. The memento of Sarao Takase."

"Why? What do you mean? This whole thing is giving me the creeps. Wait a minute. You can't fall asleep on me now."

I brought him another glass of water, and said emphatically, "Here, drink this. Then you'd better explain yourself."

Otohiko nodded and took a sip. He said, "You know, I realize that you probably don't want to remember all this stuff about that guy."

"That guy? You mean Shoji?"

"Yes. It's gotta cause you a lot of pain, and besides, you're not interested in my dad's books anyway, right? Not like before. That's all in the past, right? You're different from us. We're still obsessed by it."

"Who do you mean by 'us'?"

"Me, and Saki, and . . ."

"And your girlfriend, right?" I asked.

"Yes. For us, it's like time has stood still. You've gone on to other things since then, but we've just gotten buried in it."

"There may be some truth in what you're saying, but I know that Saki thinks it's something worth spending time on. I don't know about your girlfriend. But I would be lying if

I said that I'd forgotten about *N.P.* It's been on my mind ever since then, and I'm happy finally to have someone to talk with about it—you included, of course. That's the truth."

"So you've been caught up in it all this time, too, huh? Doesn't it get you down, though, having us hanging around?"

"It would if I thought that you were using me," I said.

"Don't be ridiculous. Trust me," Otohiko said.

"Then it's fine with me."

"All three of us feel so trapped and all alone. We regard you as someone who can help us escape. I think that's what's happening. I feel like you're the one who can change things."

"You think so?" I didn't know what to think. "Is there some threat to the manuscript so that we have to make a copy of it?"

"No, I don't think so. It's just that mementos are irreplaceable, so just to be safe, we'd better copy it."

"Let's do it then." I wanted to reassure him. "But why do you all still feel so strongly about this? I mean, Shoji has been dead for years, and your father died a long time ago. Why do you think it's so tragic still?" And I thought, but didn't say, and why all the melodrama?

"I'm not obsessed with it. It's her. She has some magical power."

This somehow made sense to me. "You're talking about your girlfriend now, right?"

"I think you're going to meet her soon," Otohiko said, "and then you'll get mixed up in it too. That's the kind of girl you are."

"What would put an end to all this?" I asked.

"When we all get old, really old, then it will naturally resolve itself, I suppose."

I laughed at this. "Oh, come on. It can't be that bad."

"I'm still a little worn-out from the trip."

"I guess so."

The sound of the rain made me feel a bit uneasy. I had felt all along that I was getting drawn into some strange psychological space. It was this pressure, something blocking my throat, that same oppressive atmosphere that I remembered from my family when I was little. Thunder rumbled somewhere off in the distance. Rain streamed down the window, and the streetlights appeared white and blurred through the glass. In the depths of the night, even Saki's smiling face seemed too distant, and I felt that I could depend on no one.

"You turn out to have a much more abundant sense of curiosity than I had imagined."

"I try not to get too anxious about things."

"Right. I should just relax too, and let things take their course."

"You'll be better off that way," I said, though I was far from clear about things myself. Silence. The sound of rain. The deafening roar of the storm. I stared out of the window, and listened quietly. Otohiko started talking.

"I really like Japan."

"Why the sudden pronouncement?"

I thought that he was sleeping, so his voice startled me. I turned and saw him looking at me, his eyes wide open, not a bit sleepy.

"I love these cherry blossoms."

Was he so very drunk that he had forgotten the season? It was summer, for heaven's sake.

"What made you think of that?"

Otohiko stared out the window for a moment.

"When I first came to Japan, it was a really rainy spring, and I didn't like it here at all. The weather got me down. But then one day, I saw some cherry trees from a taxi and they looked absolutely gorgeous. It was raining so hard that I could barely see out the taxi window. Plus, there was a chain-link fence between me and the flowers, so it was like I was seeing them through two different filters. But even that hazy view of a cloud of pink flowers made me understand the allure of Japan, with cherry trees blooming like mad all over the place in springtime."

"Nice story."

"I still feel a little like an outsider here, but when I was in Boston, I always dreamed of coming back to Japan."

"I see."

He was restless and defenseless. That wet hair, the brown curls, reminded me of a dog—or maybe a prince? He made me think of that notebook of Shoji's.

After that, Otohiko fell asleep and started snoring loudly. His snoring and the rain combined to a deafening level. Somehow all this noise felt quiet to me, a profoundly moving silence. I covered him with a blanket.

I succumbed to my own sleepiness and went in to bed after dawn but I hadn't been asleep long when Otohiko came into my room.

"I'm sorry to have bothered you like this."

"Don't worry about it," I replied groggily. "It was no trouble at all."

I opened my eyes and saw Otohiko's smiling face there before me, white in the dim, early morning light.

"I really made a spectacle of myself. I'm sorry. I'll be going now."

He looked like a figure in a dream to me as he walked away from my bed, his head bowed from the pain of his hangover. I heard the door close, and while I thought of getting out of bed to lock the door, I was so tired that I just couldn't. I closed my eyes and thought about what a strange guy Otohiko was.

The rains soon ended, and summer finally arrived. The hot clear weather continued for many days, and Otohiko's visit seemed like a distant dream. That was the way he had appeared, and that was the way he had left. I still hadn't made a copy of the manuscript and hadn't mentioned anything to Saki. In fact, the days passed as if nothing at all had happened.

That afternoon, I was in an excellent mood. I had taken advantage of the vacation and slept till noon. After doing some laundry and hanging it out to dry, I snuck in a nap out on the porch. When I woke up, I decided to go to the bank, so I put on an outfit to match my mood—a shocking pink T-shirt, and shorts, and a pair of white leather sandals. I like summer because it's the only time when you can go out dressed so casually. All I took with me when I left was a vinyl purse just large enough to hold my wallet. I felt so ecstatic when I got outside and saw that bright blue summer sky and the intense sun.

It was past three o'clock so only the ATM was open. No one else was there, so I slipped into the white boxlike space, put my card in the machine, and started punching buttons. I listened intently to the computerized female voice of the machine, then stood waiting for my money to come out. I never even noticed the clamor of summer sounds that flowed in through the door when it opened. As a matter of fact, I wasn't even aware that someone had walked in through that door. I realized something was strange only when I sensed that someone was standing right behind me. There was no one else waiting for the machine so I couldn't figure out why the person was crowding me like that. The next instant, I felt something hard being shoved into my side, just like in a stickup scene in a movie.

The thin voice of a woman said, "Don't turn around. Just hand over the money."

From the start, I felt certain that it wasn't a real thief, that it had to be a crazy person. The lobby echoed with the sound of the bell indicating that the cash had come out, and I grabbed the bills nervously. The machine thanked me.

"Just kidding. These are just my fingers in your back," she said with a laugh, and pulled her hand away.

I felt so absolutely certain it was Saki that I almost called her

N.P.

name. It's so strange. But it wasn't her. I turned around only to find a complete stranger smiling at me. This frightened me even more. I will never forget the moment when I first looked into her eyes. She glared at me as if she were going to squeeze the blood out of me. Her gaze was absolutely pure and transparent, like Sirius sparkling high up in the dark night sky, like a good dry martini beaming with pure light inside a cocktail glass.

Do you know what I'm talking about? I was gripped with fear when I saw those eyes—the eyes of a newborn on the face of an adult. How does someone with eyes like that see? And what kind of mind did she have? Definitely a strange person. I had never seen anyone like her. She was not a raging beauty, nor was she really cute, but I felt drawn to her anyway. I sensed a glimmer of animal instinct, a lump of primal intellect. I looked at her for a long time, and took her all in. She had long, black fine hair, and was skinny and tall, almost gangling, with veins protruding from her neck. She had full lips and her tight white blouse stretched across small, firm breasts. Her shorts revealed surprisingly shapely thighs and calves. Lemon yellow flip-flops on her bare feet, and red polish on her toenails. Well, at least she shared my love for the summer. I could tell that from her clothes.

"We're dressed like we're sisters, aren't we?"

"Who are you?" I asked.

55

"Sui Minowa," she gave her name. "And you're Kazami Kano."

"Yes, I'm Kazami, but I still don't know who you are."

"Oh, come on. You must know," she said with a friendly smile on her lips. A skinny arm reached out to me, just like one of the extraterrestrials in *Close Encounters of the Third Kind*.

I said, "I'm sorry, I still don't understand."

She grabbed my right hand and pulled me toward her. "Let's talk in my car."

"Hold on." I struggled to free myself of her grip. Despite her friendly, gentle smile, she had a firm hold on me and would not let go, and her hand felt abnormally hot.

"I'm not going anywhere with a stranger. Let go of me."

Her grip loosened slightly for a second, but then she came back at me insistently. "You do know me. You've known me for a long time."

A phrase that I had heard a lot recently.

"But I've never met you."

"Didn't Otohiko tell you about me?" Special delivery. So this was his woman. I was about to say something, when Sui spoke again.

"Otohiko's my stepbrother."

"What?"

That took me by complete surprise, and I was speechless.

I finally understood the one thing that the twins, otherwise so completely frank and open, had been secretive about.

"No one told me."

"I wonder why they hid it from you. Maybe because I used to go out with Shoji? And because I gave him the ninety-eighth story of *N.P.*, and he died because of that? And because it's weird that Otohiko and I are together now?" she asked with seeming innocence.

I was in shock. "But the two of you are related! Are you really Sarao Takase's daughter?"

Sui nodded.

"So was your mother Japanese too?"

"Yeah, I guess Dad liked Japanese women. My mother lives in the States, but she is Japanese. I haven't had contact with her for years, though. Don't you want to hear more? I can drive. Look, here's my driver's license." She pulled it out of her pocket and flashed it in front of me. "I'm not lying to you."

I believed her about the license, but felt doubtful about how safe a driver she would be. She pushed me out the bank door, and over to a red Familia parked at the curb. The bumper was all banged up.

"How did it get so bashed in?" I asked, pointing to the bumper.

"I ran into somebody. But that was a long time ago." She laughed and pulled me closer to the car.

"Get in."

I said, "Some other time, thanks."

I needed some time to think things through, and I really didn't want to be dragged into her car and taken away just like that. Her long hair smelled sweet, like a little child's, and those big sparkling eyes looked so forlorn under the shag of bangs. It scared me because I felt as though I could fall for her.

"At least let me take you home," she said as she unlocked the car doors. She plopped down in the driver's seat, and then, with a sweet smile, ordered me to go around to the other side. I got into the car, but told her, "Thanks, you can just drop me off down at that big intersection up ahead." I pointed down the street.

All I could see from the inside of that hot car was a long road, shimmering white in the summer sun. All the buildings and trees shone too. The two of us sat there in our shorts and sandals, with our pale legs stretched out in the sun, and it felt for all the world like the beach.

"It's like we're at the beach," Sui said to me, and a shiver went down my spine.

She turned out to be an okay driver after all, and I realized that she just acted spacy. She seemed calm and grown-up as she drove, her hands firmly on the steering wheel. I relaxed a bit. The hot sunlight glared in through the windows, but the ineffective air-conditioning didn't even bother me that much. I felt a little happier. I also thought that I might want to see her again sometime. But then, when we neared the intersection, and I started to thank her for the ride, she cut me short and said, "I'm not stopping." She sped up, and I watched the familiar intersection fade into the distance behind me.

"Stop the car."

Sui didn't even look at me. "No way. I finally have you, and I'm not letting you go."

"What the hell is going on?" I said angrily.

Sui shook her head and muttered something. It wasn't the answer I wanted.

"Maybe other people will fall for your games, but not me. I won't stand for this drama," I said, as the car sped farther and farther from my apartment.

She said, "Really? You seem to be enjoying it."

That shut me up. I didn't say another word, and just sat waiting for her next move. It was quiet for a long time, and amazingly, she just kept on driving without saying a word.

"I've been waiting to meet you for so long and I just wanted to talk. All right? We can just talk awhile. Maybe I didn't go about this in the right way, but I haven't hurt you or anything, have I?"

"Tell me more." I smiled.

"I just have so much on my mind, and wanted to talk with someone who would understand."

She smiled peacefully. At last I realized that Sui had been as tense about our meeting as I was. A realization like that makes you feel that it's okay to talk and spend time with someone, even if the first impression was bad. I decided to give in to her wishes.

"Okay. I understand. At least I think I do."

I sat in silence, thinking, for a while longer. I thought about the notebook that sat open on my desk, and the window I'd left open, and the cup of iced barley tea that I'd started to drink, and the laundry drying on the line. Somehow, I missed my apartment—intact, yet abandoned, like that ship, the *Marie Celeste*. I longed for myself as I was before I had met Sui, because I didn't know when I could ever go back.

I said to Sui, "I understand that you want my manuscript of the ninety-eighth story. Don't you have a copy?"

She shook her head.

"Do you want to see the translation?"

She didn't answer my question, but instead asked where I wanted to go.

"The beach, maybe?"

I said, "Anywhere is fine. You decide."

"Okay, I know a park where there's a nice pond. It's

actually more like a small lake," she said, and then she answered my question. "You mean the one that Shoji was doing? Yeah, I liked the original, but I'd like to look at the Japanese translation to see what he did with it."

"When were you going out with Shoji?"

"Don't get upset. It was long before you were with him. We got together after I came to Japan, and first met Otohiko. As I told you before, I introduced him to *N.P.* I gave Shoji the ninety-eighth story and asked him to translate it," she said. "I'm sorry."

"It's not your fault, but then I do blame you for introducing me to that book." I smiled at her.

"You were meant to read it."

"Were you with Otohiko in Boston?"

"Yes, for two years."

"It's none of my business, I know, but why did you come back when you did?"

"I don't really know myself. I wanted to stay there, but people change their minds all the time, don't they?"

Her car was boiling hot inside, which seemed a strange contrast to the cool scenery flowing by outside. My brain felt paralyzed, and I couldn't think straight. I told her that the air-conditioner was too low and turned it up. The cold air blasted out onto our kneecaps.

"I had a good time in Boston. It's kind of melancholy, but

really beautiful. A fantastic place to escape. But of course the problems that existed between us didn't change, even though we were there. And then we ran out of money, and we started talking about what the next step should be. He wanted to break up, and go back to Japan, but I thought that I would just stay there. And I told him I would, but then I ended up coming here, too."

"Did you know that he was your stepbrother at the very beginning?"

"I might have known."

"What do you mean, you might have?"

"I fell in love with him, and so I kept telling myself that I didn't know, and then I got to the point where I really didn't know what our relationship actually was. That might seem strange, but it's the truth. I'd wake up in the morning and think, oh my God, this guy is my brother. Or is he really? I was totally confused."

"I can see that."

The stream of cars on the road around us seemed like a river that was transporting us to an unreal world.

"I knew that you were dating Shoji. Otohiko spotted you with him at that party and told me who you were. Ever since then, I've wanted to meet you. I was depressed about coming back to Japan, but I felt a little better when I remembered that you were here."

"Oh, yeah?"

"Here we are," Sui said, and pulled the car over. It was a big park where I'd never been before. I peered through the front gate at a mass of trees. It was dark like a forest.

She said, "Let's go for a walk."

We walked through the dense grove of trees that stood just inside the entrance of the big park and emerged by a pond shimmering under the blue summer sky. Nearby, a man was selling that kind of Popsicle we used to eat when we were kids, so we decided to get a couple. The vendor pulled out two from the ice chest on the back of his bike and handed them to us.

"Are you girls sisters?" he asked.

"Sure." We laughed.

We found an old wooden bench and sat down with our Popsicles.

As Sui had said, the pond seemed more like a lake. The trees far on the other side towered high, like mountains, and the surface of the pond looked clear like a mirror. Children rambled down the gravel path on their bicycles, and people with fishing poles sat quietly on the shore. On the small beach nearby, mothers watched as their children played in the sand. Sui drew her knees up to her chest and gazed out at the high clouds, not at the water.

"You know, I don't understand why you two just didn't want to stay in Boston. Was there some kind of visa problem because of your Japanese passports?"

"I guess that was part of it. I don't know. I just got all mixed up after a while," Sui said, leaning her head to one side as if it would help her to remember. "Originally, we went to Boston because we wanted to escape from this weirdness about being related and to have a change of scene. We felt so passionately about each other that we decided to go away together, just the two of us. At first, it didn't really bother me, but Otohiko couldn't let go of it. He grew up in a good home, you know.

"I liked Boston, I really did. We used to take walks down by the river, and we'd go to the library together, and go to bars, and down to the harbor to watch the boats. We were so much in love. But then, I don't know, somehow we both got kind of stressed out, and I kept waking up at night. I felt awful when people would ask us if we were married, or when I saw old, happily married couples and stuff.

"I felt like I was in exile, and even that was okay, but then it got to the point that when I reached out to hold his hand, he would just glare at me with those dark eyes and not respond. And I thought, why can't he just smile instead of staring like that? But it didn't get any better. I couldn't feel close to him anymore, not even as a sister. It was worse than being strangers, and that was that. You know what? This is the first time I've really thought about what happened to us then. And I slept with Sarao Takase, too."

"So, you mean the woman in the story . . ." I started to say. Sui finally looked over at me, and nodded.

"That's right. The woman in the ninety-eighth story is me."

"Now it all makes sense to me. So do you feel attracted only to men you're related to?"

"No, not at all. At least with Shoji there was no blood relationship."

"That's true."

I nodded. When a dead person's name is spoken, I always feel like that person becomes part of the scene before me. Then, in particular, when I suddenly heard Shoji's name as I sat in that park, all the things around me accommodated his figure—the rustling trees casting their long, cool shadows, the summer air so thick and sweet that it was almost like fog, the sparkling, shimmering surface of the water.

I smiled and said, "When you put it that way, you and I are related somehow, too."

"We'd really be sisters if you slept with Otohiko," she said mischievously and laughed.

I replied, "Nothing like that's going on now."

I had no idea whether she was worried about that happening, or whether she wanted it to happen.

"So how come Otohiko talks about you like you were some kind of monster? Like you were going to devour him or something?"

"He believes that if we're together, fate will control us, just like in some old legend. I'm sure that's why. Silly boy."

"It's so peaceful here."

"Yeah, it really is."

We sat quietly and listened to the sounds around us—birds singing, children's voices, a bell tolling in the distance.

Sui said, "Did you read the ninety-eighth story?"

"Yes, I did, and I liked it, especially the ending."

"Oh, me, too. I always start crying when I read the end of that story. I mean, I hardly ever saw my father, and he was nuts and very weird, but at least I know that he loved me. And just like in that story, he told me that he didn't know that I was his daughter when we first met. He did say that he thought I looked like my mother. But my mom used to have sex with men for money, so—who knows?—he may not even be my father. But my eyes do look exactly like his, don't you think?"

She looked into my eyes when she said that. A chill ran down my spine. Her eyes were deep and dark, like the bottom of an old well.

I nodded and said, "I've only seen him in pictures, but it's true. Why don't you get your blood type or genes tested and try to find out if he's really your father?"

"I've thought of doing that. Then if they can't tell who the father is, I could be Otohiko's real girlfriend instantly. But, you know, then I have the feeling I would end up being overwhelmed by the newfound freedom and drink myself blind or something. And what happens if I find out that we are related? That would be even worse. If I don't get tested, then at least I can say that I don't know for sure, and that can be my out. It's like trying to decide whether to get tested for AIDS.

"People are just so weak," she continued. "Like me, I was raised in a terrible environment and have seen a lot of appalling things in my time, but, in the end, I still believe that people are fundamentally good. And also extremely fragile. In my experience, people who work at acting inhuman will suffer the consequences in the end. That's what happened to my father. Or maybe there is a God. Who knows?"

The blue sky looked incredibly deep to me. I felt so swept up by the beautiful blue that I felt tempted to ask her why they didn't just stay together until they got tired of each other, and not worry about what other people thought, just like in a romance. I felt so drawn to that blue, I thought it might be possible to live like that. But as with any troubled love, they, too, have probably seen skies like this a million times, and made a million promises as well.

"You've had a rough life, huh?"

"Yeah, that's for sure."

Sui grinned widely at me with her big mouth. I thought, dammit, I might have just fallen in love with her. She moved me, as though we had been talking like this forever.

She said, "Everyone has been bewitched by it, Father included."

Surprised, I asked, "You mean by the story? Do you think that I am, too?"

"Sure, it's just like a chain letter, and always has been."

"It's all in your mind."

"No, really. Don't you feel like you've known me forever? And Otohiko and Saki too?"

I nodded. That was exactly how I did feel.

Sui looked at me, a little calmer this time. She looked detached, as if she were looking straight through me to the sky. "Some people would call that a curse. I'm sure of that."

I nodded, without a word. The wind blew, calling up tiny waves on the surface of the pond, as if in response to her overwhelming silence. I suddenly realized that she and Otohiko might kill themselves together. Love suicide was a definite possibility. If things went on like this, they probably would do it. I hated the thought that I might have met them in order to witness their death.

Sui said, "Let's go," and stood up.

"Okay."

I followed Sui, scratching the mosquito bites on my legs. She looked cocky and slender like a pet dog, as she walked along proudly.

On the way home in the car, I remembered that phone call, the one at the office, with no one at the other end, and asked her if she had tried calling me. She nodded and kept driving.

I asked, "Why did you hang up when I got on the phone?"

She smiled sheepishly and said, "I just wanted to make sure that you really lived in town, that you really existed, for that matter. And then when I heard your voice, I got tense and hung up." She laughed nervously.

It was extremely bleak on the way back, and lonely. As we rolled past the white buildings of the city and the dusk sky, I felt that I understood everything that she said very well.

"All of us are so strange—me included. I was a character in a book, and now I've come out of the book and am talking and walking. . . . At the same time, it seems like the real me has become part of the book."

"That's not a good sign," I said.

She smiled.

We parted at the intersection where she was originally supposed to have let me off. After I got out of the car, Sui said good-bye, but then just drove straight away without even a glance in my direction. I felt disappointed at her coldness, and started toward my street without looking back, but then I heard a car honking. I turned around to see that she had made a U-turn and stopped at the light on the other side of the street. She rolled down her window and waved good-bye, a big smile on her face. Beneath the red sky, her beaming face looked like some sort of tropical fruit. It was hard to believe that I had just met her. I felt as if we had been together for a long time. She felt so familiar to me, like a childhood friend. Talking with her was so easy.

On a backstreet near my apartment, I spotted a sliver of moon in the evening sky. I gazed up at it, and thought of the three of them. Then, I prayed, like a child, that Otohiko and Sui would not kill themselves.

"Oh, you know what, I met Sui and we got along fine."

After a moment of stunned silence, Saki said, "Did you just say what I thought you said?"

We were sitting around in my office after lunch, being lazy. I smiled awkwardly, stood up, and then went over to the refrigerator to get another glass of iced barley tea. Saki just sat there with a smile on her face. She had on a yellow sleeveless dress and was sitting in the professor's chair with her feet up on his desk. I had become quite used to seeing her like that. When we first met, the gray sky of the rainy season loomed outside the office window behind her relaxed figure, but now it was really summer.

It was vacation time, and hardly anyone was around. We could hear water splashing and voices from the nearby high school swimming pool. I sat twirling the ice in my glass and sipping tea. The sound of the air-conditioner bugged me, especially since it didn't work very well.

"What do you mean 'got along fine'?" Saki asked. "She wears me out."

"Oh, she wore me out too, but I enjoyed it," I replied.

"How much did she tell you?"

"Siblings, incest, Boston, coming home." I grinned.

"Well, then she told you the whole damn story, didn't she?" Saki let out a loud laugh. Her white shoulders shook, like a sunflower. "I wasn't hiding anything from you, you know. I just thought that it had nothing to do with you and me, and, besides, it's not exactly the stuff of light conversation."

"I realize that." I said, "Don't the two of you get along?"

"I guess not. I mean, my mother hates her with a vengeance. After all that Mom's said about her, I don't know how we could ever be friends. And if we were friendly, it would seem hypocritical somehow."

"I see."

"I've met her mother a couple of times when she came over to talk about money problems and stuff."

"When you were little?"

"Well, actually, we first found out about them after Otohiko was an adult. And then the two of them got involved."

She laughed nervously.

"It's so embarrassing, all this stuff in my family."

"I can imagine. My way of looking at the world is so nearsighted. If no one said anything, I'd probably just live like I do now year in and year out, and feel complacent about everything around me. Plus, I don't see that many people. Something is definitely missing—I don't know what, maybe compassion for people who are suffering, a sense of adventure, interest in other people. . . . Yeah, so I really feel for you."

"Are you trying to console me?"

"I know I wasn't very clear." I smiled and asked, "What's Sui's mother like?"

"Hopeless, absolutely hopeless. Sui hasn't lived with her for a long time. She probably had already lost touch with her when she started hanging out with her father. A couple of times, her mom came to our house and tried to weasel money out of my mother. She would sit down and tell my mother the most incredible things about herself, like that she drank way too much, or that she had contracted VD, or whatever. So I never even knew that Sui was related to us, or that this kind of thing actually happens until after Otohiko started seeing her. It blew my mind completely, and I couldn't very well tell Mom. But you can't stop love."

"Is that what you really think?"

"What?" Saki looked at me, her eyes wide with surprise.

"That love will take its course, no matter what."

Saki nodded, "Yes, I do."

"But doesn't it repulse you physically?"

"No. I mean, I would never ever do anything like that with Otohiko, because we grew up together, but he had never even met Sui before. Plus both of us have strong feelings about our father, because he left us and we really resented that. But then we were fascinated by his fiction, and the rest. I know how he feels. That ninety-eighth story is fantastic, don't you think? It's so romantic and surreal, and it's the best story in the collection. I would fall in love too, the way that story, and Sui, and Father all came together."

"You really surprise me. I had the impression that you were too proper for that kind of thing."

"Who, me?"

"That's what I thought."

Saki smiled at me and said, "It takes time to get to know someone. You've got to give other people the benefit of the doubt."

"Oh, I do," I said with a smile.

"I'm still afraid," Saki said, "that they might commit love suicide."

She had sensed the same thing about those two. I nodded in hearty agreement.

"You saw it too, didn't you?"

"Definitely. I think that they want to die. If this goes on

any longer, they will get even deeper into it, and the probability that they will resort to suicide will be even greater. That's my feeling about it, at least."

"They're okay now," Saki said in a low voice. "This is cool. I feel like we're talking about some big secret, the way our voices echo in this big office."

"It *is* a big secret!" I smiled.

"It's not that big a deal. Let's go have coffee."

"Okay."

We got up and left.

The moment we walked outdoors, brilliant sunlight rained down on us like the flashes of a million cameras. For a moment, everything looked dark, but then I could see the usual summer landscape. I smelled the fresh grass on the empty playing field. From the high school next door, the wind brought sounds of baseball practice—the clink of the metal bat, the clapping and cheering.

"The wind feels good," Saki said. I looked over at her. The wind had swept the bangs off her broad forehead. I felt very strange. Translated into words, I was feeling wonder at the fact that a month ago I had barely even met this woman, and now we were friends. She was born in a foreign land. But inside, it was more than that. I felt so deeply moved that my chest ached. It took my breath away.

As we passed between two classroom buildings, I looked up and saw a neat little square of the sky, and floating inside a very thin white crescent moon. I could also see clouds drifting by. It was utterly gorgeous, that view that only the two of us could see. I thought about that as we walked slowly across the playing field.

Later that day, it started to rain for the first time in a long time. I recalled that wet night when Otohiko had visited me. By evening, the storm had picked up almost to typhoon force, and thunder rumbled all around.

I sat in my room, listening to the rain pounding on the pavement. Occasionally, a flash of thunder would light up the sky. It wasn't even five o'clock, but it seemed that night had already engulfed the world.

I had just finished a translation job. I really didn't feel like going out in the rain, but I needed to make a copy of it by the end of the day. Reluctantly I closed up the notebook and stood up to leave. Then, it suddenly occurred to me that I should make a copy of Shoji's translation at the same time. It wasn't just because Otohiko had asked me to make one. I myself decided that it would be good to have some extras. The day might come soon when I would show it to Saki and Sui.

I got out my precious manuscript, and put it with my translation into a vinyl bag so that they wouldn't get wet. I put on my jacket and went out. It was raining hard outside, and I ran into a nearby convenience store where there was a copy machine.

I propped my umbrella up next to the machine, and went to work. The inside of the store was too bright, and the sky outside was black. The wet road, car headlights flashing rainbow colors. The green light of the copier shone on my face. Every time a new customer came in the door, the sound of the storm outside flooded in over the store clerks' voices. The wet floor glimmered white in the light of fluorescent bulbs.

I was copying with such concentration that when I finally finished, it felt as if I had accomplished something. I paid for the copies at the front register, and then stuck the bundle of white paper back into my bag. Outside, the rain had slowed a little, and the western sky glowed with streaks of orange. The sides of the buildings around me were dyed in the brilliant light.

I decided to stop for some tea before I went home, but then it happened. I had barely taken a step away from the store entrance when I heard someone run up behind me at a terrific speed. Then, something heavy hit me in the back of the head, with a loud thump. It didn't hurt as much as surprise me, but I fell to my knees. I noticed something on the ground next to me. It was a plastic bottle of oolong tea, like the kind they sell in the grocery store. I turned around, only to see those familiar white legs planted firmly on the sidewalk before me. Slowly, I looked up at her face.

Firmly, I said to her, "What the hell are you doing? That hurt. What were you thinking of?"

It was Sui. Her face looked peculiar. It was pale and trembling with tension, but very out of it.

"Look what you've done! I'm all wet."

I picked up the bag and slowly stood up. I looked her straight in the eyes, and she burst into tears and wailed loudly like a baby. And this was only our second meeting. My God. Passersby all turned and stared. Embarrassed, I pulled her into a garage nearby. The sound of the rain beating on pavement faded away once we were inside, and my ears filled with Sui's sobs instead. I stood there in the smell of wet cars, feeling mortified and outraged, for all the world like a mother whose child was having a temper tantrum in public. First she knocks me down, and then she pulls a stunt like this.

"Explain yourself," I demanded.

Sui snapped angrily, "You made those copies because you think I might do something with the manuscript. And you lied to me too."

I was in shock. I asked her what she meant.

"You thought that I was going to steal the manuscript, right?" she said in a nasal voice.

"You're wrong," I started to say, but then realized that I

sounded like I was trying to defend myself. I felt annoyed that I had been so easily caught in her trap.

"You have no right to criticize me for copying something that is mine."

"But you told me that you were my friend!" Sui said sharply. Her whole body spit out these words, and her face flushed red from the effort.

"I never said that!" I yelled, and my voice boomed with surprising fullness through the small garage. I sounded insistent and loud, as if I were trying to make myself understood to someone standing a long ways away. I could see Sui's body tremble, though only for a moment. Perhaps I had said that I was her friend that day. Even if I hadn't communicated that with words, perhaps I had let her know with these eyes of mine, or my smile. Maybe that was proof enough for her.

I reached into my bag and pulled out the copies of Shoji's work and handed them all to her. She accepted the bundle of paper quietly and then attempted to say something. Her face looked fresh, as fresh as the moment when words come into being inside a person. But then, before she could speak, she covered her mouth with her hand and looked down.

"Are you sick?" I asked. She reminded me of Otohiko that night, and I realized how alike they were. Both of them could succeed with daring feats like this, but then they could barely make it through an ordinary day.

Sui moaned, and a trickle of blood oozed out between her fingers. A red drop hit the sidewalk by her feet, like a drop of ink on a white sheet of paper.

With a blank look on her face, Sui said, "I guess I got a nosebleed from all the excitement."

"Well, why are you looking down if you have a nosebleed? Put your head back."

"Okay."

Sui tilted her head back, her hand clutched at her face like the hand of a corpse with rigor mortis. I peeled it away and gave her a handkerchief.

"Thanks," she said, her voice muffled by the handkerchief she held up to her face. She stared silently at the ceiling, her eyes red from crying.

She seemed so wretched to me, and my heart filled both with revulsion and pity. What had her childhood been like? I had met all sorts of people in my day, but Sui was completely in her own category. The dark colors that emanated from her, the overpowering, nearly oppressive presence that even she could not control. She was like a hydrangea beaten down by the rain.

I said, "Come to my place and wash that blood off of your face."

Sui nodded. I slung my bag over one shoulder, but I didn't bother with the umbrella, which had broken when I fell. I took Sui by the hand and guided her along, since she still had her head tilted. The rain had slowed to a drizzle.

Had she been following me? And for how long? I didn't even bother to ask.

I took her into the apartment and turned on the light. She just stood there. I gave her a washcloth and told her to wash up. She turned the faucet on full force and splashed her face with water. She looked refreshed and awake when she came out of the bathroom, and that made me a little tense.

"Will you give a copy to Saki too?"

Her bangs were wet, and she looked as if she had just gotten out of the pool.

"Yes, I intend to."

"You don't have to," she said, her face expressionless.

"Recently I've been feeling like all three of you have been parking your emotions at my doorstep," I said. Not to mention showing up at my place. "There's nothing wrong with it. I just feel weird."

"But it's kinda fun too, don't you think? This space we're in is strange. All of us like it, and we always have."

"You mean the world of that story?"

"Right." Sui smiled.

"It's got kind of a Gothic tone, but, at the same time, it's amazingly serious, and romantic, and escapist. In the end, I think that Saki's approach makes the most sense. She objectifies it and then makes it the object of her research.

"But not you. You make it real." I smiled.

"Yes, I live it," she said, "but it still doesn't help me to figure out what I should do in the future."

Sometimes when I'm feeling down, I wonder what life would have been like if my parents hadn't divorced, or if I hadn't lived alone for this long. What would have happened if I hadn't become aware of the potential of language then, or if I hadn't fallen in love with Shoji? Would I still be me? Would I be a free agent?

"I can't imagine a life without a story," Sui said.

I poured her a cup of coffee. She took a sip and said, "I bet, I just bet that you have actually gotten over Shoji completely, and you are observing us, as part of a little project for your summer vacation. You're watching us up close and personal."

She said it normally, with nothing between the lines.

"How did you know?"

She smiled broadly at me. I was just joking, but then when I saw her smile, I felt like what she said was true.

I was going to visit Saki's (and Otohiko's) apartment. I'd made more copies of the manuscript to take with me, because I'd given all the extras to Sui. It felt invigorating, under the summer sky, to think of sharing, so simply and easily, this memento.

Although I saw Saki daily at work, I had no idea what kind of place she lived in, and imagined various settings. Maybe her place would be cute, with a country decor, or sophisticated and bluesy. On my way there, I guessed it would be one or the other of those two styles. I would see it in a matter of minutes, anyway, but I still kept on wondering. Consulting the detailed map that Saki had drawn for me, I walked along the scorching hot road.

I took a left, and another left, and beyond the third left turn, down at the end of the street, I saw a Western-style apartment building. It had spearmint green walls, and a small courtyard, and looked just like the sort of place where Saki might live. Ivy twined around the gate in front. It kind of looked dark and rundown, though, and had the feeling of a retreat. I climbed the outer stairs, and knocked on the door of their apartment, number 202.

I heard Saki call out my name from inside. "Kazami? Is that you?" She opened the door for me.

"Did you have any trouble finding the place?"

"Not too much."

"Otohiko's not home."

I nodded and went in. I had guessed right. It was cute, though not childish, with a dark carpet, and lots of English books crammed onto the shelves. To my surprise, it seemed like someplace by the sea. The nautical touch was subtle but definitely there. She had an old rocking chair, and a leather couch, and, in the kitchen, a potbellied stove. Lots of different liquor bottles filled the cabinet. Somehow it seemed like the galley of a ship.

"Do you like the ocean?" I asked.

"Oh, Otohiko does. He wanted to go to a marine college."

"Why didn't he?" I asked, peeking into his room. Inside, I saw boots for wear on a sailboat, a picture book of tall ships, and even the steering wheel of a ship hanging on the wall. I didn't know about this side of him.

"Well, there was this woman, you see," Saki said with a smile.

"You have explained it with great clarity and brevity," I said. Saki brought me a glass of ginger ale.

"There's gin in it."

"We never drink at school, do we?"

"We practice moderation."

We sat on the floor and sipped our drinks. The mixture tasted sweet and strangely delicious.

I said, "It was hot on the way over."

I could feel a buzz from the gin as my body cooled off.

"Nice place."

"Thanks. You'll have to come to our house in Yokohama someday too. It's a traditional Japanese house, with lots of rooms. It was kind of a shock when we first came to Japan. That was the first place we lived here, and I had a hard time getting used to the interior. That place blew my mind."

"I bet it did. I'd like to see it sometime."

I wondered what it felt like to move to a country where you didn't grow up. I had thought about that often since my sister got married. Do you become a character in a story native to that land, or do you, somewhere in your heart, want to return to your homeland?

At that moment, the door opened and Otohiko came in. I don't know what it was, but he always struck me as interesting, and somehow strangely unique. I could tell that he had confidence in himself—not completely, maybe, and with a little desperation mixed in. I found that attractive. I liked his face too. He was a man with a story.

"I've come to visit," I said.

"Welcome."

He still seemed slightly embarrassed about his late-night visit. I felt strange. *N.P.* is just a book, for heaven's sake. Even if you become obsessed with the book, eventually you should be able to chase it out of your mind, unless you're tragically flawed.

But what was the deal with these people? Take Sui, for example. At first, she seems real to me, as she talks, shakes her hair off her face, smiles with her full lips, spills food, has gooey nosebleeds. She reacts to what I say in real time. But then reality starts to creep away, and everything goes fuzzy, and it feels unreal to me. It's been that way since I met her. She *is* N.P.

I don't know if I've fallen for her, or for Saki, or for the situation itself. Sometimes I even feel attracted to Otohiko. This makes me very uncomfortable. In this type of situation, with a small group of people and heightened emotions, you start imagining things. But, even so, I wanted to be there. I wanted to hear his story. He had this weird serious streak in him.

When you've fallen in love, broken up, lost a loved one, and start getting older, everything seems the same. I couldn't tell what was good and what was bad, what was better and what was worse. I simply didn't want to have any more bad memories. I wished that time would stop, and summer would never come to an end. I felt very vulnerable.

Saki brought out some cake and offered some to Otohiko. He shook his head and said that he'd just have coffee.

We sat on the floor as if it were tea time and sipped our coffee. This felt weird too, probably because it was the first time the three of us had sat down together in one place.

"Did I tell you? Sui attacked me the other day," I said. "It was on that really rainy day. Did she tell you?"

"You met her?" he said with surprise.

"Yeah."

"Hmm." He sounded like he could picture the whole scene.

"So, what did she do to you?"

"Oh, it was no big deal. She was just mixed up about something."

"And when she gets confused, she gets totally confused."

"You didn't know that we'd met?"

"No, not until just now."

Saki had been sitting there quietly, drinking her coffee, but she finally spoke up. "Excuse me for being so rude, but I have a question."

Otohiko said, "Go ahead."

"What's it like to sleep with someone you're related to?"

Saki looked so dead serious when she said this that I couldn't help laughing. Otohiko smiled too.

"That was an extremely rude question. You surprise me," he said.

"But this was the perfect opportunity to ask, and I hardly ever see you anyway."

"I actually have never really thought about it, but I guess I always feel guilty, and I would have a hard time explaining it to anyone else."

"You've always been that way. You've got to have a good reason before you can so much as kiss someone," Saki said.

"That's for sure," I teased.

"Can you ever have sex without having a good reason to?" Otohiko asked.

"It seems like your big sister has been harassing you about this for a long, long time."

He nodded in affirmation.

"I don't put pressure on you. It's just always been fun teasing you."

I sat there thinking how strange it all was. They were behaving just as they had at that party, to my eyes.

"Well, that's all in the past. To get back to your question, it's been years since I first met Sui, and we hardly do stuff like that anymore. We're more like brother and sister."

"That *is* what you are!" Saki said, and we all laughed.

I then gave Saki her copy. She hesitated at first. In contrast, Otohiko was eager to take a look and immediately started reading. "This translation is great. It's really good. You have your work cut out for you if you want to do better than this, Saki."

Saki nodded. My heart pounded fast.

At dusk, Otohiko glanced out the window, as if he needed to check the time. He stood up and told us that he was going out.

I guessed that he probably felt like seeing her when the sun started to set. Perhaps, the contrast between the darkening landscape and the opal dusk sky reminded him of the lightness and darkness in her. The memory of her white cheekbones compelled him to go and search for her before she disappeared, as the bright sky at dusk is swallowed up by the night. He was fascinated that she both needed him and rejected him.

"Tell Sui hi."

Saki and I watched him go. Saki shook her head and said, "Those two are hopeless." Then she and I went out to get something to eat.

I could tell even on the phone that he was drunk. He only calls me, his own daughter, when he's had too much liquor.

"How've you been?"

"I'm fine. How are you?"

It was Saturday evening, and I certainly hadn't been expecting his call. Father doesn't have a family anymore because the woman he left my mother for ran away with another man. There are people like that, who have no fear of failure and are constantly starting from scratch. They never appear to be at peace with themselves, but then it's no wonder. People like that may claim what they do is right, but you can tell from their faces that they have many regrets, like they've been banished to some dark alley. That's what my father was like, and his lover too. I have a hard time with such people, and I had difficulty being friendly and smiley-smiley to them, even as an adult.

"I'm feeling good."

"Yeah? You're not lonely?"

"I'm used to being by myself, and my son is living nearby."

"My stepbrother, huh?" I said. "Our family's pretty complicated too."

"What do you mean 'too'?"

"You know what I mean."

"There are lots of families like this. Everybody has some kind of problem, almost everybody. There are many kinds of people in this world. You realize that, don't you?"

"I guess so."

He said, "If you don't like the alternative, then get married and stay that way."

"I don't feel confident enough even to try."

I think a lot about invisible wounds, about mental illness that runs in families, about kids whose parents get divorced, all those distortions in life.

You can spend your whole life just trying to get by. I wondered what would ever bring my father satisfaction.

"Have you been drinking a lot? Do you drink every day?"

"Yeah, some sake. But you like to drink too."

"It's in my genes."

"Guess so."

"Dad . . ."

I started to say my parting shot, something that I'd wanted

to tell him since I was little—wouldn't he really rather be living a straight settled life than be a drunk?—but I stopped myself.

"How's work?"

"Work is going very well."

"That's nice."

I knew that it would be even more of a shock if I asked him if he'd ever wanted to sleep with his daughter, so I didn't.

"Talk to you again soon."

"Okay. Good night."

I had been so careful about my every word that I felt exhausted, as if we'd talked on the phone for hours about everything and nothing at great length. I could remember times when he still lived with us and we had ordinary conversations. I remembered them vividly, as if they were real, but I could no longer make them real. My body felt awkward, like when you skate or ski for the first time in a long time. This is what time does. I was still a child inside when I thought of him. I knew, however, if I were to meet him, he would see me as the female adult that I am, a woman who looks like my mother. It would never work.

Sarao Takase had wanted more than anything to die. Listening to the tone of my father's voice then, I understood why. Did he think that having a lover was the most important thing in life? And did he, like my father, dream that such love would last forever?

"Why don't you come over?" said the voice on the other end of the line.

At first, I thought that it was Saki, but then I realized that it was Sui's voice. They were indeed sisters.

I said, "I've got some work to do."

I definitely was busy, working alone at sorting through piles of files in the office. That building was like a swimming pool at night, even in the daytime, with its shiny dark hallways and the smell of oxygen.

"Otohiko's not around, and I'm bored. Plus, I have something to show you. Come over later if you want."

She seemed very familiar, even her gloomy side; I did feel like seeing her again. The sky outside my window looked like a swath of chambray dyed a brilliant blue. I felt happy.

"Okay, when I get to a good place to quit, I'll come over. What should I bring?" I said enthusiastically.

"You're in a good mood. How about some éclairs from S Bakery?" she said, and then told me how to get to her house.

★ ★ ★

That evening, I followed her directions, and was surprised at how far away she actually lived. I had the impression that her place was near mine, but even by bus it took about twenty minutes. She lived alone in an apartment house, square and white like a block of tofu, on the edge of town.

I finally got there. As always, I tried to guess the decor before I arrived. What I didn't imagine was that it would be the nearly empty apartment that it turned out to be. There was absolutely nothing to show her taste. She had a refrigerator, of course, and kitchen utensils, which were so nondescript that it seems more appropriate to call them implements. There were no rugs or cushions on the floor. A single table sat in the middle of one room, and the sliding paper door had one small hole in it. I stood there staring at it, and she presented her excuse in a strangely matter-of-fact way, "I've been thinking of fixing that hole, but it's just too much trouble."

Only the bookshelves gave a sense of her. Mounds of old English books, coffee-table books, photography books, Dickens, Henry Miller, Camus, Yukio Mishima, old paperbacks, fashion magazines, comics. It looked like a mosaic.

I said, "It's so empty."

I realized that she had no affection for her home. To her, it was probably just a box. That's what it looked like.

"I'll get you some iced tea," she said and disappeared into the kitchen. The tea she brought me tasted like mud.

"How is it?"

"Just awful."

"Someone at work gave it to me. I'll make some coffee after you finish that," Sui said with a smile.

We sat at the kitchen table and ate the éclairs. The wind chime that hung on her porch rang noisily. I felt uncomfortable. The feeling of unbalance about her had the effect of setting people on edge. But that was also part of her charm. After I leave her, I always feel as though I've forgotten to tell her something important, and then end up wanting to see her again.

"What did you want to show me?"

"Oh, yeah. Here, a token of my appreciation."

She handed me the bundle of yellowed paper that had been sitting on the table.

"What's this?"

"Actually, it's the ninety-ninth story."

I was surprised.

"There's a ninety-ninth story? Does anyone else know that this exists?"

She didn't answer.

"Does Otohiko know?"

She nodded.

"And Saki? And Shoji?"

"No, not them. At least I never told them. I don't think that Shoji knew."

She looked a little sad, but I couldn't tell why.

"May I read it?" I asked, and she nodded.

I started reading it. It was a handwritten manuscript in English. I remember that, while I was reading it, Sui sat gazing out the window. I could see her only out of the corner of my eye, but, strangely enough, what I recall most vividly about Sui even now is her profile at that moment.

I immediately understood why the ninety-ninth story had remained a secret. It didn't hold together as a story, perhaps because of Takase's state of mind at the time. It was discursive, a rough sketch. The sentences were threadbare and somehow pathetic.

Repeatedly, the narrator describes a scene with the wife he had abandoned, and his children. In his dream, the narrator goes to see his family at home. He watches them from the front door, and from the ceiling. He peeks in at them from a crack between the sliding doors. He cannot speak to them. Only the children notice something, but their mother tells them that they're just imagining things. He stands there, his face pressed against the window, staring at them for a very long time. The whole narrative consists of repetitions of this same incident.

I said, "It's too sad."

This was behind the scenes right before he died. And he described Otohiko and Saki just as I had seen them at the party, pure and always smiling.

"It makes me feel so wretched," Sui said. I realized that she saw the story from a completely different point of view. I could tell from her eyes.

"That's how you feel?"

"On the one hand, he loved me as a daughter, and, at the same time, he loved me on a merely sexual level, as a woman he'd picked up somewhere. I always get jealous when I read it, and it hurts so bad."

"Love is love. It doesn't matter what kind it is," I said. "I think that the ninety-eighth story is fantastic. The man's love for her as a daughter and as a woman are one and the same, and this powerful feeling expands to fill the whole universe. It's uplifting. You're the one who people should be jealous of. That's the best story in the book."

"You think so?" she said, grinning widely. "Well, he's dead, anyway, and so is everything he wrote. There will never ever be another story after this one."

"I was wondering if it would be nice to give a copy of this to Saki. I'm sure she'd feel a lot better," I said.

"Maybe. Then maybe we could become friends. I would consider giving it to her if it would change our relationship. But when I think that she would read this and feel happy, it really upsets me."

"I can imagine."

"And I can't stand the thought that Saki might publish a book with commentary on Takase's unpublished works, and appendices, and all that. Is that too mean of me?"

"No, that's only natural," I said, because that's what I thought.

"Whose side are you on, anyway?" Sui asked with a puzzled look on her face.

"I'm not on anyone's side in particular."

"That's what I thought you would say."

"Well, then, why did you ask?"

"You're strange."

I felt very happy, because it seemed like a great honor to be called strange by Sui. I couldn't help but smile.

"I was just wondering, did your father give this to you?"

"Yes. He wrote it in my room and then he died."

"Yeah? It's the real thing, huh?"

"It's creepy to have this written in his own hand. But when he gave it to me, I was just a child, and I didn't know any better. And I certainly never dreamed that I would still be holding on to it as an adult."

"For sure."

It seemed weird to me. It was a story from another dimension, more foreign than a foreign land.

Sui said, "You know, I have something that I've been meaning to give you for a long time. I've made up my mind. I'll give it to you now."

I smiled and said, "Let me guess. It's the one-hundredth story, or maybe the hundred-and-first story, right? That's it, isn't it?"

"I've kept this the whole time too, 'cause you weren't at Shoji's funeral." She went into the next room, opened the closet, and took out a small wooden box.

"What could it be? A piece of ivory?" I said. That sounded funny, even to me.

"Close," she said. "Go ahead. Open it."

It was light. I lifted off the lid. Inside, on a piece of cotton, was a chip of something so white that it made me shiver. Actually, it had a yellow tinge to it, which seemed very familiar to me. It was like her house, a color with history. A thousand sensations and thoughts flashed through my mind.

"Is this a piece of bone? Is that what it is?"

"Yes, it's Shoji's."

Sui smiled self-consciously. I wondered if this were something to be ashamed about. She, in fact, seemed proud of herself.

"You know, at a funeral, how the mourners gather the ashes, after they come out of the crematorium? Well, when I was doing that, I stole a bit of the bone. It was still hot. I felt really nervous," she said with a smile, her cheeks flushing red. I sat there in a total state of shock, but then I decided that talking might help me to snap out of it.

"And this is all that's left of him."

"I'm glad you feel that way," Sui said.

I wasn't happy to be feeling that way at all, but I did feel deeply moved, whether by her almost unfathomable attempt at kindness, or by the bone from Shoji's body.

"Thank you."

The little pine box felt heavy in my palm. I tried to ignore the weight, but every nerve in my body focused on it, and my fingertips seemed to be getting numb.

"Where's your job?"

"I work at a hostess bar part-time."

"What do you do? Sing karaoke with the customers?"

"Yeah, I do that too."

"I see. Not to change the subject or anything, but your place is so empty."

Sui smiled. "I find it relaxing."

Her apartment seemed like a coffin. The streetlights shone in the darkness outside her window.

Sui said, "Stay a little longer, won't you? I like it when you're around."

I squirmed a bit when I realized how much she needed me.

"Okay." I couldn't stop thinking about that charred fragment of bone.

That night, I got together with a friend from high school and drank a lot. I hadn't seen her in a long time. I got pretty drunk, not so much that I couldn't walk, but enough to give everything halos.

On my way home, I ran into Otohiko. This happened a lot, because we both hung out in the same part of town. I'd often pass him on the street or notice him browsing in a bookstore. We'd usually greet each other and then go our separate ways.

That night, however, I was in a daze and didn't even notice Otohiko until he came up and greeted me.

"Oh, if it isn't Otohiko!"

"Hey, you're drunk!"

"Let's go have tea."

He laughed. "Kazami, it's two o'clock in the morning."

"Let's go to Mr. Donut," I proposed. "They'll still be open."

"It's too far. I know, let's buy some tea from a vending machine and drink it here in the street."

"What a cheapskate!"

"It's something you can do only in summer."

"That's true," I said.

Summer was already half over. In just a matter of weeks, it would slowly fade out. I felt sad.

We bought some barley tea from a vending machine we found. The two cans rolled down and landed with a thump. The cans looked really big to me. Then, Otohiko and I sat down in front of a store there on the street. Cars whizzed by at a tremendous speed. Every time a truck passed, I could feel the ground shake.

"Sitting on the street like this is cool. You can't forget where you are," I said. "You can really feel the night."

"For street people, this is the way it is all the time."

"That's true. If you lived this, it would become normal."

Time stopped in this space apart from daily life. I sat there watching the cars and passersby. It all looked strangely clear to me. The streetlights that stretched in a row far down the road towered closer to the sky than usual. The headlights flashed in many colors, and I heard the car horns, and a dog barking in the distance, and all the sounds of the street, and people's voices and footsteps, and the sound of a shutter flapping in the wind. I felt the humid air, and asphalt still warm from the daytime, and summer's distant smells.

"How're you feeling?" I asked.

"Terrible." He reached over and squeezed my hand hard.

"That hurts."

"That's how bad I feel."

"What a baby! How much do you love Sui?"

"Let's see," he said, taking a sip of his tea, "I love her so much that every woman I see on this street looks like her. That's how much I love her. Wasn't there a song like that? So I plagiarized."

"But nicely put," I said.

"But it's no good between us, and we can't fix it."

"It's okay."

"I'm scared."

Time stopped. Perhaps God in his grace glanced down upon us then. It was that peaceful, for an eternal moment, in the valley of the night. The night resembled Sui.

When I thought about that moment later, in the light of day, it didn't seem so monumental. But when it came upon me, the touch of darkness was undeniably vast and pure.

"When I was living in the States, I had a good friend whom I often went sailing with. He was quite a bit older than me. One time he came to visit me in Boston, and he and Sui and

I went out for drinks. Sui had never met him before, but they got along fine, and she played the role of my steady and faithful girlfriend perfectly. Sometimes, the presence of a third person smooths everything out and gives you the illusion that everything is as it should be."

"I know what you mean." I didn't say that it only happens that way if the relationship is extremely shaky to begin with. The wind whistled through the valley between the tall buildings in which we sat. I felt like a fish able to see the world only inside this tightly enclosed space.

"I couldn't fool my boating partner. It was strange how perceptive he was. He could see things exactly as they were. After Sui got tired and went home, he said something to me. He said, That woman of yours scares me. He told me that he'd seen women like her in the ocean. They would call him down into the depths. This would happen when he was feeling distracted from his work, or when he couldn't concentrate, or when he was feeling weak. A man only sees them when he's young. And then you know what he told me? He said, I've seen a lot of dangerous women like that, and they all looked at me like your girlfriend did tonight. They bewitch you with their eyes, sometimes without any goal in mind. She made me think of those women I saw in the ocean. I knew exactly what he meant."

I nodded. "You understand everything, don't you?"

He nodded. A midsummer's night, very late. When I closed my eyes, it seemed as though I could hear footsteps walking stealthily away. I sat motionless on the sidewalk, listening to that for the longest time.

I sat with Sui on the banks of a river out on the edge of town. We were eating some bread.

Sui said, "Summer's almost over."

We sat there watching the river flow by. Small glistening waves covered the surface of the water.

"Yeah."

The blazing sun had warmed up the concrete that we were sitting on, and everything looked bright white. The sound of the rushing water resounded in my ears.

"I can't even open my eyes, the sun's so hot. It's like I'm sleepy or something," said Sui, and she leaned against my back. Her head was small and hot, and felt like that of a tiny bird in the palm of my hand.

"The heat's oppressive," I agreed, and didn't move, partly because I had eaten too much and felt stuffed, and partly because it was too much trouble.

"Oh, I'm so sleepy. See, my hair looks blond when you hold it up to the sun," she said to no one in particular.

"There's a breeze."

The wind felt good. On the green grass all along the dyke, people were playing catch, walking their dogs, and picnicking with their families. The sky spread vastly above the river and the bank opposite the river and beyond, all the way to the houses and buildings in the distance. It was an intensely blue sky that promised to suck us up. My body felt heavy, and my arms and legs were infused with the heady scent of the grass. I didn't care what happened, about anything, past or future. The hot air tightly enveloped my sweaty body. I closed my eyes, and the inside of my eyelids looked red. The sun's rays burned my skin.

"I love this! But it's too hot. I get the feeling that a spirit might come to see us, if we called. Who would you like?" Sui said with a chuckle, her cheek still pressed to my back.

"Shoji," I said with a smile. I took a sip from my bottle of juice. I could feel the cold sweetness trickle down into my gut.

"I shall call him," Sui said and then fell silent. Still leaning on my back, she said, *"I'm sorry, Kazami."*

I wanted to tell her to knock off the joking, but my voice froze. Even though I knew that she was teasing me, my whole body, from where her head rested down, felt intensely cold. I broke out in a sweat. It was her voice, all right, but, coming through my back, it had the sound of a different realm.

"I'm sorry that I couldn't go to the beach with you. I know that I promised I would. And sorry about not returning the books and your wristwatch."

My body was paralyzed with such fear that tears welled up in my eyes. My body hardened, stiff like a rock. At last, I managed to say, in a weak voice, "What are you doing? Sui, how did you know?"

I turned around and looked at her, and she stared back blankly. The bright sunlight revealed the freckles that covered her pale face. What an insubstantial girl.

"I was just talking nonsense. Are you crying? I'm sorry."

She pressed her hand to my cheek. It was so hot that I felt dizzy.

I said, "I'm okay. Just a lot of memories."

Sui came and sat beside me, and then she put her hand on one knee of my jeans. Her eyes squinted against the bright light, as she gazed silently out at the river. Under the intense sunlight, something just clicked, and it turned out like that. Just as if it was supposed to have happened that way. This is how I made sense of it as I sat watching the river. I stared at the water intently, and felt that I was flowing by. The water ran perfectly clear, and I could see fish darting around. The grass beneath my hands gasped for air.

"I'm sorry," Sui said again. She looked straight at me and smiled. Every feature on her smiling face was in clear relief, and she reminded me of close-up pictures I had seen of children in India, smiling with all their hearts.

I got together with my mother for the first time in what must have been several months. She called out of the blue, and invited me to lunch the next day. My mother didn't have any more children after my sister and me. Her husband (I never lived with him, so that's how I think of him) was a magazine editor. It was his first marriage, and he, of course, had no children. They had invited me to live with them, but I decided not to. Sometimes I regret having refused them, or feel guilty for having turned them down. My regret comes from my understanding that the longer you delay independence, the better. And when I hear her lonesome voice on the telephone, guilt overwhelms me.

It was noon, and the restaurant was crowded. I ran in ten minutes late and spotted my mother, who was already drinking a cup of tea. She wore a navy blue suit and was nicely made up. She sat gazing out the window. Somehow, she looked like a widow, but then Mom had had that air about her for many years.

"Hi, Mom," I said. She turned and smiled.

"You look like you've lost some weight," I said, after our food had come.

"Maybe I did lose a little. It's been so hot this summer that I haven't been eating much."

"Have you been busy?"

"Oh, yes. In fact, I have an appointment with a client after lunch."

She smiled at me. She looked older than she did when we lived together. For the most part, I live my life as if time didn't matter, but when I see Mother, I feel as if a time machine has suddenly transported me into a well-defined future. The changes in my mother made me keenly aware of the passage of time.

"Are you doing any interpreting work?"

"Oh, once in a while I get farmed out, but at my age interpreting is just too much of a bother. I only accept jobs from people I feel obliged to."

"So you're doing written translations?"

"That's most of what I do."

"You just keep on doing that, don't you?"

"Why do you say that?"

"I've been doing a lot of part-time translation jobs myself

recently, and I keep wondering why I've fallen into this line of work too."

"I don't think you're really cut out for translation, you know that?"

"Why? Because I'm not accurate enough?"

"How can I describe it? You're weak, not really weak, but too kind. You think that you have to be faithful to the structure of the original sentences."

That had been bothering me about my own translations lately, and I thought of quitting.

"That sort of thing is inevitable no matter how hard you try to separate yourself from the text. You're so sensitive, Kazami, that it's going to wear you out."

"So there's no way around it?"

"That's my opinion. Shoji wasn't cut out for that kind of work, either."

"You have a good memory," I said. Mother nodded—of course she would remember him.

"Once you get too involved with a text, it's difficult to let go of it or create it in another language. That's what I think. Of course, if you don't like the book to begin with, then you have to suffer through it," she said with a smile. "I know how Shoji felt, though. I've been translating for more than ten years, and sometimes I get very weary. Translating exhausts you in a special way."

When the waitress brought us dessert and espresso, we took a break from our conversation about translating. I felt strange because it was the first time in a long time that Mother had talked about her work, or what was on her mind.

"You become so involved with the writer's style that it starts to feel like your own. You spend hours every day with it, and then you end up feeling that you alone had created it in the first place, and then your thoughts fall into sync with the author's, and that's very peculiar. Why, sometimes I get so far into the author's thought processes that I feel no resistance at all. I become unable to distinguish my thoughts from hers, and sometimes I find myself thinking the way she would, not just about the book, but about my own life, even when I'm not translating. Particularly if the author has a very strong personality, a translator gets drawn in so tightly, much more so than an ordinary reader would."

"And that happens to you too, even though you're an old pro?"

"Yes, and in fact I've been thinking about that a lot recently. When I first started doing translation, I really wasn't any good at it. It was right after the divorce, and work didn't distract me from my troubles at all. Sometimes I couldn't sleep at night, wondering how I could make a living and raise you kids at the same time. And then I had to sit down and struggle with someone else's writing all day long. It was a terribly lonely time for me. I felt as if I was going to get crushed by all the demands on me. But I found ways to distract myself, and to not think at all for a while."

"By taking care of us?"

"Are you kidding? Raising children is one of the biggest challenges," she said with a smile. "For me, it was *kendama,* those wooden ball-and-cup toys."

"You did what?" I said with surprise.

"You know, *kendama.* It seems funny now, but at the time I worked at it very seriously. Don't you remember me doing it?"

In the back of my mind, I had a vague memory of the eerie click-click of wood striking wood from inside my mother's room. Sometimes I'd hear her doing it at night when I got up to go to the bathroom.

I laughed and said, "Oh, I thought you were pounding a nail into a voodoo doll."

"I was the champion in my grade school *kendama* contest, you know! Even now, I get it out and practice, but in those days I was at it constantly. It's amazing how I became so wrapped up in it. But, you know, I don't think that you can find as good an escape as that with video games, or even television, or books, or drinking."

"What's the difference? If you're really into something, that's all that matters, isn't it?"

"I'm not sure. I have the feeling you get the same effect from a sauna, or swimming, or standing on your head, or even cutting your nails. Perhaps it has to be something physical. But then maybe that's just me. Even with the type of translation work I do now, I sometimes need a total escape, in a place without a story."

A story. I felt as if I'd heard that term before somewhere recently. Sui had used it.

"You've got to become totally absorbed in whatever it is you're doing, like chanting sutras, or meditation or something."

"Absolutely."

"Both Shoji and I liked stories too much, that's why neither of us were cut out to be translators," I said. I wasn't sure that I could lose myself totally in *kendama,* or cutting my nails.

"You always absorb everything around you, down to the last breath of air. Remember when you lost your voice? You are always so sensitive to the people around you, even though you don't want to be part of the drama. I guess that's why you're strong. But no matter what, I never, ever, want to see you cry again like you did when Shoji died. You're a strange girl, Kazami, you're a little like your father."

"He called the other day."

"How is he?"

"In pretty bad shape."

"Oh yeah?"

"You never change though, Mom. You're still so young."

"You think so?" she said with a smile.

Physically, she looked much older every time I saw her, but when we'd talk, I would catch a glimpse of something inside her, her true personality. It was this part of her that had resisted the passing years, and sometimes I felt I was talking to that young woman inside.

"So, have you been enjoying yourself these days, Kazami?"

"I'm having lots of fun."

It was true. That made the sense of regret even keener, that this time in my life would soon be a thing of the past. I felt as if I could understand a little of what my mother had been through, and the feelings she may have had at different times. I wasn't a child anymore, and this made me feel awfully lonesome, and utterly alone.

I liked Sui a lot, but we got together only when she called me. I never called her, because I knew that if I didn't set limits on our relationship, she would start hanging around me all the time. If that happened, I'd become so dependent on her that the idea of life without her would be unbearable. That's the kind of effect she had on people.

The couple of weeks of midsummer were strange. The sun shone so strong and bright, it seemed it would never set. People changed, things happened under that eternal sun. I wasn't aware of it but autumn was shooting out buds. Then suddenly one morning the wind turned cold and the sky looked so high, a reminder of the passage of time, dashing my hopes that summer would never end.

I couldn't see it, but things had changed. Sui called me constantly. When I heard her voice on those hot summer days, I felt as if my soul were rotting from the inside of my ears. I felt positive that something was coming to an end. Then Otohiko's face would appear in my mind's eye, just as it had looked that moonlit night as we sat by the road.

Late one night, Sui called. I could tell from her voice that she was pretty drunk.

"Otohiko's gone to bed already. He's so mean," she said.

She's just being oversensitive, I thought.

"Well, he was probably sleepy. So what?"

"I've always been around people who love to sleep. My mother used to fall asleep drunk, and I would watch her late into the night. He was like that too—Father, that man, Mr. Takase, what should I call him? He would talk a blue streak in the dark, about his hopes or regrets, or complain about things. After proposing some solutions to the problems—that was always the final section of his monologue—he'd fall asleep. I would just lie there wide awake, thinking about art, freedom, rebellion. I did more thinking than he did, I'm sure. That's the advantage of insomnia, you know. People who go to bed early always complain that the night is too short, but, for those of us who stay up all night, it can feel as long as a lifetime. You get a lot done."

"Why don't you have a drink and go to bed, too," I suggested. She seemed to be in a lot of pain.

"I have been drinking."

I didn't detect any anger in her voice, nor did she seem on the verge of tears. Her manner struck me as empty, like the forced smile of a woman whose love has gone sour. I'd felt that a lot myself, so that I could picture her mood clearly in my mind. Men usually don't notice such nuances of feeling. Or maybe they do notice and then react by falling asleep (itself a form of abandonment), just as Otohiko had done to Sui.

"How can you talk so loud with Otohiko asleep?" I asked.

"Oh, I'm not calling from home."

My heart skipped a beat.

"You're at a pay phone?"

"Yeah, one close to your house."

I wasn't surprised. I had nothing else to do, so I made up my mind to go down and meet her.

But first I said to her, "You seem to think that I have nothing but free time on my hands."

"Human relations never used to be like this, you know that? In the old days, everyone had time for other people, and were much more friendly," she said with a laugh.

"You're at the pay phone on the corner, right? I'll meet you there in a minute, and then we can go for a drink."

I grabbed my purse and left right away. As I walked along the dark street, it occurred to me that Sui might not be as strange as she seemed, after all. She might be perfectly healthy. Actually, she didn't seem mentally unstable to me at all, but in fact pretty together. What was it that attracted me to her? Was it her self-sufficiency, her ability to stand on her own? Or the unique cause of her suffering, something that set her apart from other people's pain?

Sui stood outside the phone booth she had called from. She looked like a slender willow branch waving in the summer breeze, except that she was wearing sunglasses.

"What's the deal with the sunglasses? It's dark, you know."

"My eyes are all red from crying," she said in a nasal voice.

I noticed that she was clutching a bottle of wine in a brown paper bag, and I said to her, "If you'd thrown that at me, I'd be dead now."

"Don't worry!" she said and laughed loudly. I felt relief when I saw her lips curve into a smile. I hate it when people cry.

"I was drinking this wine on the way over."

"Wow! Right out of the bottle, in a brown paper bag and everything? You probably think you're like some super-cool media star, right?" I teased, and gave her a gentle pat on the shoulder.

"Wrong. I drank it from a paper cup." She laughed again.

"Yuck. I don't like my wine that way." We were having fun.

"Too bad. I wanted to tell you about this place where I've been drinking. It's incredible. Want to go there with me now? Or would a bar be better?"

"No, the place you just mentioned sounds great. Where are you talking about?"

"You'll love it! There's no one around," she said. "I bet you've been there before a bunch of times."

"Where would that be?" I thought for a while.

"Follow me."

I enjoyed being out that evening because it was the weekend and everyone and his little sister seemed to have come out on the streets, like at a festival time. I love summer nights. Some guys came up and talked to us, I suppose because we were dressed in skimpy summer clothes and were rambling along like we had time on our hands, but we ignored them and just kept walking.

"Don't you think the end of summer is fun? The energy level is really high. That Otohiko's sound asleep when there's so much going on," Sui said. The red T-shirt she was wearing looked good against the dark night.

"It's no wonder. Anyone who hangs out with you has got to be that way in order to survive."

"I guess you're right. I shouldn't think that the universe revolves around me, right?" she said with a smile. Whenever I said something about them that I would usually say to a normal couple, I was always left with a bitter, poignant after-taste in my mouth.

"Where is this place?"

"Right near the intersection with the big supermarket. You know the place? Around there."

"You've got to be kidding," I said. "That's close to where Shoji's apartment was."

"Would you rather not go?"

"No, it's okay. I haven't been there for a long time, and I'd like to see it again."

When we at last turned onto the narrow street right off the boulevard, it was so dark that it made my head reel.

"This is it."

The apartment building rose high into the darkness. On the front hung a white banner announcing that construction was in progress. All of the windows were dark. I couldn't tell if they were going to renovate or add more stories to the building. So, this is what happens.

"I came to see him a couple of times when he lived here, but we never made love because he said he didn't want to hurt you. Nice guy, wasn't he?"

"You make him sound like he was."

I looked up at the darkened building. There was a dry cleaner on the first floor, and you entered the apartments from the side of the building. The rest was a lumpy, gray, three-story apartment building with no elevator. Shoji's apartment was on the third floor. The view of the street that you could see from his window was always narrow and peaceful, whether morning, noon, or night. It was so calm that I felt as if I were looking out of a window in Shoji's body. I slept well in those days—content in a way I will likely never be again.

Sui said, "When I was over here a while ago, I walked around and discovered that you can climb up all the way to the roof. I was crying the whole time, you know."

"That's neat," I said, "just like in a mystery novel."

"Just wanted to see if I had enough guts. It seems like it would be as scary as hell if you found yourself up there alone."

Then we walked into the pitch black, silent entrance hall. The sound of our footsteps echoed in the engulfing darkness. I recognized the stain on the wall of the staircase landing when I caught sight of it in the moonlight. I had a vivid memory of that spot only, as one often does with childhood memories.

When I was a teenager, I dreamed of living here. I didn't fantasize about getting married, or even moving in. Rather, I just wanted to stay in his apartment and never go home. As I climbed up the stairs and saw the dark doorways, a vivid image flashed into my mind and I couldn't chase it away. A bird's-eye view of Shoji's apartment. The dish cabinet inside the front door on the left. The avocado green refrigerator. Scraps of writing and photos tacked up on the wall. The bed by the window. The glass jar filled with coins. The big parakeet that he kept secretly.

I felt strongly that everything would still be there, same as it ever was—like when the spirits of dead people return home during the late summer *Bon* Buddhist festivals. Like the garden in my paternal grandparents' house where I visited only during summer vacations. I have a vivid memory of the plants and flowers there, but I will never see those people again, nor will I visit that house again.

"I feel like I'm drunk even though I haven't had any alcohol. Doesn't my voice sound strange to you?" My voice trembled in the dark stillness.

"You're drunk on your memories," Sui said nonchalantly.

We reached the landing at the top of the stairs. I had been up on the roof only once before, that time, to fly a kite. The door to the roof had a lock on it. Shoji had a copy of the key made for himself, so that we could go up there and fly some kites we had made ourselves.

"There's a lock on the door."

Sui grasped the rusty doorknob and rattled it wildly, like a gorilla in a cage.

"Breaking and entering! You're making too much noise!"
I yelled.

"Don't worry," she said, slamming her body against the
door. I couldn't see her face but it scared me that she was so
intense. Finally, she cried out, "I got it," and pushed the door
open with a screech. We emerged from musty old air that
reeked of paint and thinners into the fresh night air.

"It's nice to be outside again," she said. A broken water
tank sat in the middle of the roof. A clear view of the skyline
spread out all around us and it was so still that it reminded me
of city lights reflected in a lake. We sat down, and Sui brought
out her bottle.

"This wine's not cold," she said, handing me a cup, "and
I hope you don't mind the paper cup."

"Paper cups get all soggy when they have wine in them,
and it's gross."

It was red wine and actually tasted pretty good.

"Want some cheese?" Sui said, as she pulled some out of
her bag and handed a chunk to me.

"Nice party."

"Not bad, eh? Summer is the only time you can drink
outdoors, except for when the cherry blossoms are out in the
spring," she said. It sounded like something that Otohiko
would say.

"You both like the great outdoors, don't you? Otohiko and I had an outdoor tea party like this not so long ago."

"I always want to go outside after we've had a fight and I'm feeling all cooped up in the apartment. Once we get outside, then we make up."

"Another tip from the wise one," I said. We could hear the faint sound of cars passing on the street below. I shivered as the cool breeze blew over my sweaty body and blew my skirt up around my knees.

"You know what's really fun? After you've been drinking someplace like this, and then you go to a bar and just have one drink before you go home. It's something different."

"Yeah, it's really jarring to be in two such different places."

"Want to do that?"

"Okay."

"You know, I never have really had any friends. There were a lot of girls who I hung out with, but never anyone who I could talk with like this. I could talk with Otohiko, but he's the only other one."

"He's the man," I said. "Maybe that's why you were the perfect pair. You could complain, and talk about your doubts and still keep on going."

That's how most couples made a go of it anyway.

"I wonder," Sui said. "If we had a normal relationship, we may have broken up long ago."

"What was it like with your father?"

"We were poor, and I was just a kid. We lived in the city, and my mother had disappeared. I was a mess, all mixed up in the head. I couldn't tell the difference between right and wrong. All I had plenty of was energy. He was my type, and I had no notion that what we were doing was bad. I'm pretty sure he thought it was wrong, though. But I feel sure that he would have died anyway, even if he had never met me. I'm glad that we did meet, and that we got close."

"Don't you think you got too close?" I said, and she smiled.

"Maybe so. But that's what I feel comfortable with. Japan is so orderly. People have standard ideas of what constitutes good and evil. People worry too much about what other people think, but then you run into lots of mashers on the subway. And the next minute you'll meet some lady who does something so nice for you that it makes you want to cry. It doesn't make any sense to me. What a bizarre place. But I'm older now, and something inside of me is changing. I don't feel comfortable in Japan, but usually I do okay."

"I'm hearing the opinions of a Japanese who's been overseas most of her life."

"That you are," she said. "I always resigned myself to the idea that I'd wake up where I'd wake up."

"That would drive me out of my mind."

"I want to sleep in the same bed every night, in my bed at home."

"You can do that now."

She said that she wanted a life that wasn't all wildness. I prayed that she wouldn't start listing all the details of her sad and sordid inner story.

"You look so devastated. Everything I've told you is the truth, even though it may sound like a story. I'm still alive. This isn't meant for public consumption, just you," Sui said abruptly. She surprised me.

"I'm sorry. Did I look like I'd lost hope?"

"Yeah, like you didn't want to hear me saying that kind of depressing stuff." Sui smiled. Her narrow eyes twinkled.

"Have you ever really been in love?"

"I think I have, but I'm not sure. Maybe with Shoji, but he died before we had even had our first fight," I said. "You're acting a lot like a big sister to me. What's going on?"

"Everyone I've met since I came to Japan seems so insubstantial, even Otohiko. I used to think that people were supposed to be more strange, and dirty, and full of all sorts of emotions, pity and nobility, with infinite layers of complications. I really enjoy life, and being in love. I like being really feminine, and strong and weak. I think it's cool to sit and watch the moon together after we've had a big fight, yelling at each other and stuff. I like feeling different ways when we do things we do together, and crying. I always try to look good when I go to see my lover, no matter how long we've been together. It's all intuitive. It has nothing to do with logic." Sui smiled. "You've got to have a wild love affair. I'd show you how, but I'm a woman too."

"Have you ever been in love with another woman?" I asked, my heart pounding fast.

"I've had women tell me they love me, but I never loved them back. If I did, it would feel like I'd won the Triple Crown."

I laughed hard. I felt a little drunk. The sparkling lights of the city seemed to be drawing nearer.

"I do like you, though. You make me feel safe but also kind of nervous. It's a strange feeling. I think that you've rescued me. You're different," she said. "Let's have fun together. There's still some summer left."

Then she stretched out her body beside me. The sweet fragrance of her hair close by, the smell of jasmine and sandalwood. The scents of the summer night crept up inside my nose.

"I wonder what you'll be doing in late summer years from now. Where will you be?" I asked.

"I don't know."

The increasing honesty and openness between us scared me. Her gentle kindness felt like the adoration of a pet, and it frightened me. She had no notion that anyone might reject her physically. I was neither a lesbian, nor an innocent high school student anymore. I was just a woman.

All three of them smelled strongly of their pasts, when life was vital and rich. For me, being with people like this seemed like being in a flower garden that is subtly out of sync with reality. I felt that strongly. This time in my life was splendid, beautiful. But there was a limit. It couldn't last forever. I would open my eyes and wonder why I was still there with them.

The wind was strong, and a little chilly.

"There is a curse, you know," she said.

"Stop it! Don't talk about things like that when we're in the dark." There was an old clothesline lying on the white concrete floor. It was a dead space, where only a few points of light from the skyline were breathing. Is someone there, listening to us? Is he always there, always?

"After Shoji died, did you feel it?" she asked. "Didn't you feel that there was always someone else in the room with you?"

"What are you talking about?"

In fact, I had had that very sensation. The morning of the day he died, in this building.

Sui's eyes opened wide, and she said, "Ever since I was with Father, I've always felt it, even later, when I was with Shoji and Otohiko. I have this feeling of powerlessness, that I'm the tool of something outside of me. I'm always the weak one.

"I'm not afraid of anything except for that. I feel it constantly. It was in the room before Father died, too. I saw signs of it. It's the force of an evil fate and it comes from that book. Father died because of it. It makes me sick that it may be the reason that I'm alive, and that I met you, and that we're here now, doing this."

"What do you mean by 'it'? The power of that book? Your father's talent?"

I looked up at the starry sky. I thought of all the people I'd met, as I sat on the top of a wrecked building, like some ruin in a foreign land. I'm the one who's feeling that. Who am I? I can never get any further than that.

"No, that's not what I mean. My father is just ashes now, and before that—what?—a wandering Japanese person who abandoned his country. It possessed him. Even after he died, it didn't disappear."

"When you say 'it,' do you mean art, the artist's soul? Or are you talking about something else like . . ."

She stopped me in midsentence. "I mean something else. Do you get it? An evil spirit, a curse, bad karma. Bad blood, like the blood that's preventing me and Otohiko from being together."

"Are you sure? You can conquer it."

"I wonder," Sui said. "She'd better let go of it, too."

"Who are you talking about?"

"Saki. Oh, I didn't tell you. I sent her a copy of the story."

"That was quick," I said with surprise. I stood up, and was looking down at the ground far below, my hand on the railing. It was so unexpected that I felt as though heaven and earth had turned upside down.

"You told me to send it to her, and I thought it would be the best thing to do."

I turned around and saw her grinning at me. Her white shorts and white teeth stood out in the darkness.

"You should have given it to her in person," I said.

She looked embarrassed. "No, I'd feel awkward. . . . Boy, am I drunk."

She turned over on her stomach. For a while, I could see that she was building a mound of small chips of broken concrete with her fingers. Then she just lay there with her eyes closed, and that made me uneasy. I leaned down to make sure that she was okay and saw that she had fallen asleep. I shook her awake.

She rubbed her eyes and pushed herself up into a sitting position. "I was dreaming about a grave. It's bad not having anyone underneath us here."

"Yes. It's one big grave," I said. "Let's get out of here."

She nodded. We climbed down to the bustling street again, and went to get something to drink. When I look back at that night now, I know that it didn't hurt me. It seemed good, like a time when I was wrapped in something like a childhood dream.

One afternoon in late August, Saki and I were walking down the street on the way home from a movie. We had decided to stop and have a cup of tea before going our separate ways. The area in front of the station bustled with people, but somehow it seemed quiet.

We had just crossed the traffic circle, in the middle of which was a fountain shining in all the colors of the rainbow, like in a painting. Through the dancing waters, I spotted her thin face. Sui had a special air about her. You could single her out easily, even in a huge crowd of people. She walked along blithely, with an easy step.

Without thinking, I called out her name. Immediately, I could tell that Saki was mortified. Sui turned and said hello, but the moment she caught sight of Saki, her matter-of-fact expression turned into an awkward grin. She came closer to us.

"Haven't seen you in a long time. Thanks for the copy of the story," Saki said casually, as if she ran into Sui all the time.

Suddenly, Sui embraced Saki. She held her tightly in her arms, and said, "It's been too long."

Tears welled up in Sui's eyes. I realized that Sui was truly happy to see Saki. Saki shrugged her off and said, "Stop it. Let go of me." She smiled so nicely that it gave the impression that she was just being sociable. Sui released Saki, and looked her usual self again.

"You've really grown up," Sui said.

"I see Otohiko all of the time, but the only image I have of you is as a child. It's nice to see you. I can't believe how glad I am to see you."

The three of us stood there. Cars proceeded slowly around the plaza, and a line of buses stood at the stop. So many things filled the space of that very ordinary, clear afternoon. The many complications, the things that had evolved over time, the varying distances between Japan and the rest of the world. People walked right by us, and their voices interrupted our conversations, without any of them realizing all that was going on between us. It felt strange.

Why had Sui cried? What will happen to the two of them once they're forgiven one another? Although I had known them for only a brief time, I was overwhelmed by the illusion that I had been observing both of them since they were children. It doesn't have to be so complicated all of the time. I hope you all are happy. Sometimes it takes a long journey to find your biological family. The space where we stood was heavy with air and intensity.

Sui said, "You look much more like Dad now than you did when you were little."

Saki blushed. "You think so? What about me reminds you of him?"

"Your eyes, and your nose. They're just like his."

"That's what my mother says too."

"You two look alike," I said. "You look like sisters, not just half sisters."

"Really?" Sui said, and examined Saki's face. She stared at her for such a long time that I thought she would burn a hole through her. Suddenly, she smiled weakly, and then the smile turned so sad that it made me want to sigh. Something was bothering her. I'd seen that smile before. In return, I felt pain that I had known before. Finally, Sui's pleasant smile came back, and she said, "Maybe we do, here around the nose." She poked Saki in the nose with her index finger.

After we had said good-bye to Sui, Saki said, "I wonder why I never ran into her by accident like that before." She looked puzzled.

I said, "God probably just now decided that it was okay for you two to meet."

"Why? I haven't changed any."

"That's the way things go."

"It's my brother's life." Saki smiled, then said, "I worry about her. She's so forlorn, and I always have a slight feeling of regret every time I see her."

"She walks away as if she were going to disappear. I wonder if I'll ever see her again."

I turned and saw her yellow blouse receding into the distance as she walked along the busy street. She looked iike a balloon someone had let loose in the sky. We watched her go.

Even now, I cannot translate into words what happened after that. Perhaps Otohiko will be able to express it more clearly in years to come. I am unable to explain anything about that summer articulately. All I remember is the hot sunlight, and a strong sense of not being there. Of my own lack of presence. What role did I play? How did my emotions figure? I feel as if I had become the summer itself. As summer, I had a unique vantage point. I was able to watch her.

Sui. I became part of the air that surrounded Sui, and breathed in her incomprehensible sadness. I think that part of those feelings still live within my soul. Burdened by bad karma, and a soul that beckoned such unfortunate fate, Sui used all the resources she had to make her way through love. I witnessed that.

How were her father and Otohiko different? With millions of men on the earth, why did she choose her own relatives?

Sui was selective about what she believed.

There's no such thing as perfect love. If you and Otohiko break up, he will be relieved too.

Are you happy with your life up to this point? It's your fault that nothing good has happened to you.

Despite her arrogance, she was well aware that hers was a slender existence. She believed in the groans of that dubious soul, and the brilliance of her intuition.

She possessed a life force that was fundamental and un-tamed. She was like a kitten who is flung into muddy water and cries pitifully but still survives. Shoji lacked that tenacity, and people like Otohiko and I are unable to believe in it completely and remain ambivalent.

Sui realized that energy in her own way. That summer, I watched her from close up. I watched Sui.

"Why don't you come over? I'm feeling lonely," Sui said tearfully.

Not again, I thought. "What's the matter? Where's Otohiko?"

"You want to know where?"

Despite her teary voice, she let out a loud laugh and said, "You'll love this. He went to a camp."

"A camp?" I laughed too. "You mean like a camp with campfires?"

"An American friend came to visit, and they decided to go traveling together. They left about three days ago."

"All those funny things he does are just like a boy."

"Absolutely. Oh, by the way, I had something I wanted to tell you. Come on over."

"Okay. I have some time."

It was the first time I had seen or talked with her since the day Saki and I ran into her after the movie. It was early evening, the time to switch on the lamps and chase away the

144

dark blue light that creeps into the house. Nowadays I didn't really have a clear head until very late afternoon, rather like an alcoholic. I'd watch the streetlights float up in the growing darkness on the hilly residential streets. I'd have a beer, and then realize that it was a new day, and that I had been going about my daily business just like everyone else. Only then did I wake up.

I wondered if I were constantly possessed by something or other. It wasn't like the illusion of having a second self that a person with a split personality would have. Then another question kept popping up in my mind: When wasn't I obsessed by something?

I knocked on the door, but there was no answer, so I tried the doorknob. The door opened without resistance. Inside, all the lights were on, but Sui was nowhere to be seen. I noticed that the sliding glass door out onto the porch had been left open. The light evening sky looked like a picture that had been fitted into the aluminum molding of the door.

I stepped a little farther into the room and caught a glimpse of Sui standing out on the porch. It struck me that she was smoking a cigarette, something I rarely saw her do. The wind had swept her hair straight up, where it stayed.

"Hi."

She turned around and said, "Come in."

She looked like a mere wisp of cloud against the colors of the night sky. Her lips were blue from the cold, and her eyes red.

"I was taking the laundry down from the line, and I then got tired, so I'm taking a break now."

"Don't worry about me," I said, and had just sat down on the floor of the porch, when Sui suddenly let out a gasp. I stood right back up.

"What's the matter?"

"Why did you have to sit there of all places? Oh, no, you've got coffee all over you."

I turned my head and looked down, only to discover a large brown stain on the back of my white summer slacks.

I shook my head in disgust. "Oh, great. It looks like I pooped in my pants."

"Just a bit ago, I kicked over a coffeepot, but I guess I forgot to wipe it up," she said with a chuckle. "What a silly coincidence. Here, let me have your slacks. If we wash them right away, the stain will come out."

"Do you have some other pants I can wear?"

"Sure. Here you are."

Sui handed me a black cotton knit skirt that she had pulled out of the basket of clean laundry. I went into her bathroom and changed, while she tossed my slacks and some detergent into her washer.

"Sorry about that," she said, bending over to place a rag on top of what was left of the coffee puddle. "I'm putting this rag here so you won't sit in the same spot again."

"Very funny." The pleasant buzzing sound of the washing machine filled the apartment.

"Do you like doing laundry?" I asked.

"I like the sound of the machine," she responded.

"Oh, here, I brought these for you," I said, and handed her some flowers and sweets.

Sui held the flowers in her arms and said, "Lilies! For me? They're my favorite. Don't you think that they look like me?"

"Lilies don't look like anyone who claims a resemblance to them."

"Whatever you say."

Actually, I thought that they did resemble her a little, especially their strong fragrance, and the yellow powder on the stamen that stains your clothes. At that moment, though, Sui's calm smile made me miss the chance to say so, and I felt like a shy teenage boy.

Her eyes were like glass, and her pupils cold and cautious. That day, Sui felt so sweet to me, like she was doling out her lifetime's stock of sweetness. She could warm up the air, and then gently blow it out, just like a lily. She smelled of a syrup made of boiled-down despair.

"I'll tell you, though, everything feels flat now that I've given it away," she said, as she placed the vase of cut lilies on the table.

"You mean the copy of the story?"

"Yes. Strange, don't you think? That was my last hold on my childhood. When I had it hidden, I used to walk around intoxicated by my own secret. I thought that no one else knew about it. It was all unconscious, of course. I actually thought that the story increased my value as a person. What a mixed-up kid."

"That's strange. I mean, you've done fine on your own. That story was just a good-luck charm. You could go anywhere in the world and do okay—here, Africa, India, anyplace."

"You really think so?" Sui said with a smile. "Yeah, I feel as if I've regained some of my self-confidence."

I could tell that she only said this in an attempt to mollify me, and that upset me. I needed to say something to cheer her up.

"You complain a lot, but actually you're very tough. You've never gone crazy or done anything really stupid, right? I predict that you're going to end up a happy person. You have talent and a passion for life, Sui. I've spent enough time with you to recognize that. You've had a hard life, but you've got your head screwed on right."

"Thanks." The corners of her lips turned up slightly in a smile. That wisp of a smile made me remember a similar expression on Shoji's face. A tenderness that comes from resignation, and a stubbornness that will not listen to reason.

Sui said, "Talent and charm just eat a person up. I'll fall in with the crowd and die a nobody."

"A lot of things have to change first. You're just tired."

"It's been a long time since I've looked at things from a global perspective. Maybe since I met Otohiko? Since my falling-out with my mother? Since I slept with Father? Since I broke up with Shoji? Since I've been pawed by all those men at the bar? Since I came to Japan? I couldn't tell you exactly how long it's been."

"You look so tired and pale."

"Well, actually, I'm pregnant."

I was astonished by this disclosure. "When's the due date? Are you positive?"

"I just went to the doctor yesterday and that's what he told me."

"Is the father Otohiko?"

"I'm not absolutely certain, but I think so."

"That's a bit of a problem, isn't it?" I said. That was the understatement of the century.

"I suppose so. I should get an abortion, then?" she said nervously.

"What else can you do?"

"I really don't know." Sui leaned her head to one side, and fell silent. I didn't say anything right away, but then, when I finally turned to speak to her, I saw that she had her eyes closed. She appeared to be listening to the winds of another world. What world would that be? I wondered sadly.

I looked closely at her lightly freckled skin, and the pink of her closed eyelids. I felt as though I were examining a picture through a view finder, or within a frame, rather than a living being. That was the first time I had studied her face so carefully. Until that moment, I don't think I had looked properly at her face because her eyes were always stealing the show. Or perhaps it was because the color of her eyes and their light were all of her. Now, though, the color of defeat emanated from her being, in the strange shades of resignation that come over people who are exhausted from the pressures put on them.

Suddenly, Sui opened up her eyes, parted her lips slightly, and started to speak. Her face looked very content.

"This is embarrassing, but I'd like to see 'Father' once again."

"Father?"

"Yes, a man who hugs and plays with his baby, and comes home early from work, and takes pictures of it with the camcorder, and who might get upset with his wife when the baby wakes up crying early in the morning, but who never gets mad at the baby. You've got to realize that I have absolutely no confidence in my ability to be a mother."

"You want to see Otohiko like that?"

"No, not him. Just a generic father, a man who wants to be there to watch his child grow up. I don't know whether I want Otohiko to be that way. Maybe I really do, but I pretend that I don't."

I was crying. There were no tears in my eyes, no teary expression on my face, but something heart-wrenching filled my chest. It would have been rude to cry.

"But will you do this much for me?" she said with a smile. "Will you come with me to the clinic?"

"Of course I will. You know what you should do? Talk it over with Otohiko when he gets home from . . ." I burst out laughing. "From camp!"

Sui laughed too. "Yeah, as soon as he gets home from camp." The word *camp* seemed completely incongruous in the context of his life, given his age and situation. I was sure that every time I heard the word *camp* from then on, I would think of that day with Sui and smile.

"There's nothing we can do about it today, anyway, so why don't we have a bite to eat?" she said.

"Dinner sounds good. Let's go out," I replied. "Oh, but are you up for going to a restaurant? Shall I make something here for you?"

"I have some soup and bread that I made. Would that do?" Sui said, with an unbelievably sweet expression on her face. It was as if she felt compassion for me. That's what I saw in her eyes. They brimmed with compassion.

"I get to taste your home cooking?" I stuck my tongue out in make-believe disgust.

"It has poison in it." Sui laughed.

"I don't mind."

In a while, Sui brought me a bowl of thick beef stew, a hunk of dark, crusty rye bread, and a cucumber salad.

"It looks great!"

"I hope you'll like it," Sui said proudly.

"Aren't you having some, Sui?" I asked.

She grinned and said, "I don't feel like eating. Did you just say my name?"

"What?"

"Did you call me Sui?"

"Yes, I guess I did."

"Coming from your mouth, it sounds like the name of something nice."

It all tasted so good to me. I slathered the bread with butter, and gobbled it down. Sui sat sipping at her beer and watching

TV as I ate. Then I noticed that something was wrong. The room was too quiet. The sky never turned dark. The television sounded tinny and cold. The feeling of the place, the passage of time, and the walls and the floor and everything were slightly off. I had never seen Sui look so small.

How could I have known she wasn't joking about putting poison in the food?

The next thing I remember is thinking how roughly she was handling me as she dragged me along the floor. My body felt heavy and I could not move, or speak. The harder I tried to open my eyes, the more tightly closed they felt. I tried desperately to see what was happening to me anyway.

I could faintly hear Sui's voice and laughter from a distance. "I'm sorry."

I felt her hands wrapped tightly around my ankles. Her hands conveyed a forceful message that was in direct contradiction to the gentle laughter that came from her lips. I sensed colors, not words, this time, just as I had as a child without a voice. A powerful color, a deep, dark purple, surged through my legs. The feeling of her grasping on to my legs so hard that she would crush them. I sensed that she was asking for help.

I could feel that she wanted to die. Her exhaustion far exceeded what showed on her face, just as it had been with Shoji. I understood what was happening, and that's why I kept trying to tell her not to die. But, just as on that winter day of my childhood, words would not come from my mouth. Only a strangled sound squeezed from my throat.

"Die."

"You think that I want to die? Why?" Sui said, and let go of my legs. That feeling was still strong, even though she wasn't touching me anymore.

Had I been born just so I could be here with her now?

It was all over with Otohiko. Finished. And it had taken this long.

Sui's heart and soul resembled a scrambled, chaotic mosaic, but now all those millions of pieces were focusing on a single word—death. She was speeding toward it silently and at a tremendous speed.

I tried to stop her, spitting my words out like bullets: "You must be kidding. We had a good time this summer, didn't we? We laughed, and cried, and forgot everything. And I'll forget all about you if you die. That's not what you want, is it?"

That's what my heart wanted to communicate to her, but my body felt more and more like a lead block, and the words that actually came out of my mouth made no sense. "No . . . this . . . die . . ."

Sui stood up abruptly. After glancing down at me, she walked toward the door. I knew then. It pierced my heart with utter certainty, with the clarity of crystal, and the brilliance of lightning. I knew that I would never see her again.

She *is* like a lily, I thought as she walked away. I regretted that I had never told her that.

At that very moment, she turned and said, "What? A lily? Did you say 'lily'?"

I have no idea how I managed to, but I sat up. It hurt, as if my body had been glued to the floor, and I had to peel myself off. I was barely conscious. It even felt as though only my inner self sat up, as if my soul had left my body (not that I would know what that feels like). I had my eyes closed, but I could feel her standing there looking at me.

"Wow, this is just like that scene in *Fatal Attraction!*" Sui said. "How did you get up?"

I'm sure I was able to get up then because the drug hadn't entered my system completely. My body was somewhat resistant to medication anyway. What fueled me was something of a different order: Desperation; questions that had dwelled within me since childhood; all the thoughts and feelings that arose in me right after Shoji died; or the image of Sui that's been in my mind's eye ever since I met her; my feelings for Sui; Saki and Otohiko's smiling faces; regret that the summer was coming to an end. The sorrow of being alive, a sentiment Sui knew all too well. The blinding bright sunlight when I first met Sui; the glimmering surface of the pond. Her hands, her hands holding mine. The sound of her hair fluttering in the breeze. Summer, the shimmering colors that surrounded Sui, the direction her life was heading in. Grief.

"What a waste."

I think that I said this clearly enough for her to hear. Or maybe I couldn't. But she understood anyway. I could tell from her face, and her wide eyes, that she had received the energy from my mind.

"You think it's a waste?" she said, and then she came back to me. I felt her arms around me and her lips on mine. She kissed me deeply, though not for long. My mind was growing foggier by the moment, but I do remember thinking that I'd never kissed another woman like that before. As if she had read my mind, Sui smiled and said, "Now I've won the Triple Crown."

I passed out.

Someone shook me hard, and I woke up. My head throbbed with a pain so bizarre that I thought someone had stabbed me. The sharp pain completely wiped me out, and my mouth felt parched.

"What the hell happened?" I said.

"What did you drink?" It was Otohiko's voice. He looked about ready to cart me off to the hospital. I shook my head to let him know that he didn't have to, but the movement only made the pain worse. I winced.

"My head hurts."

"Do you want a drink of water?"

I nodded. As I was gulping down the lukewarm liquid, I noticed that I wasn't in my own apartment. Then it all came back to me.

"Where's Sui?" I asked.

"She's disappeared," Otohiko said. He looked as though he were about to cry.

"I know that she's gone. How could this have happened?"

I managed to sit up. Everything was exactly as it had been:

the laundry basket on the porch, my slacks drying on the line, the bowl I had eaten out of, the open window. Everything was the same, only that Sui wasn't there. I felt utterly miserable and desolate, unable even to cry, like an abandoned child, like after the festival is over. Every time I moved my head even slightly, pain would zigzag through it, and my whole body would tremble.

"What time is it?"

"Two o'clock in the morning."

"It was early evening when I got here. Sui looked exhausted, and she told me that she was pregnant. Did you know about that?" I asked.

"She told me that she might be." The words came pouring from his mouth. "She said that she wouldn't have the baby. We were supposed to talk about it when I got home from my trip. I think she knew that anything big like that would spell the end of our relationship, because it just wasn't working anyway, and we both knew it. It's a miracle that we've lasted this long anyway. I could deal with it if she really wanted to go ahead and have the baby, but I felt that she herself didn't want to have it. I couldn't make the decision for her. During our last conversation, I felt like we were saying good-bye."

"And you went to a camp?" My head hurt so I couldn't laugh after all.

"Yeah, I wanted to spend some time outdoors."

"Oh. Weren't you two using any type of birth control?"

"We were. Sui was taking the pill."

"So she might have stopped taking it on purpose, or maybe she just forgot or something."

"I think that she didn't know what she was doing, and then, without really thinking about it, tried forgetting to take it," Otohiko said, his hands in tight fists on his lap.

Otherwise, it was an unusually quiet night. The air seemed desolate like a grave. This was the sad wreckage of a broken dream.

"Would you get me some more water? My head is killing me." I flinched from the pain. Otohiko took the cup from me, and said, "Why in hell did she drug you? How come? What an awful thing to do."

He sounded angry and worn-out, exhausted from more of the same.

I said, "She was going to kill herself."

"You think so, too? I had this terrible premonition that she had made up her mind to die, and that's why I came home early from the trip. And then I get here and find that she's gone. I was almost at the point of proposing that we die together. Actually, we'd both been considering doing that for a long time. I'm sure it sounds ridiculous to an outsider, but

159

we'd been obsessed with the idea since I don't know when. But that's beside the point. I don't understand why she would do that to you. She liked you best."

He seemed genuinely puzzled, but I had it all figured out. Sui truly wanted to die, but she knew that she would have to do it before Otohiko came home. She also wanted to see me one more time, but she was afraid that I might guess her intentions. She invited me over anyway, but then, when she saw me, she panicked and didn't know what to do. Perhaps she even thought of killing me, but she decided against it. She only made me unconscious.

"I stopped her. With all my heart. I did my best to stop her," I said.

"I just hope that she gave up the idea herself," Otohiko said, his voice trembling.

"I can't tell. I'm sorry."

"I have hope. Her car's gone, and she took her bank book and a few personal belongings."

"Really?"

I couldn't think straight. I realized that I still had on the skirt she had lent me, and it was all rumpled from my having slept in it. I felt that time had passed since she left. And I felt a presence. Sui was no longer in the room, but something lurked in the corners of the bookshelf, the swaying curtains, beneath the tables. Those small, dark spots had slipped a bit away from reality.

"Maybe there is a curse, like Sui said?" I ventured.

It started raining. I could hear the faint, dark sound through the open window. The melancholy that accompanies the night swept in and filled the room. It coldly watches those of us who dwell in our bodies as we struggle through the day. The shadow of death. The feeling of powerlessness that sneaks up on you when you're not watching; the desolation that will swallow you up if you let down your guard.

"I don't know about its physical properties, but there was a feeling in the air. I always felt like we were wasting time when the two of us were together, no matter what we were actually doing. Life lost its edge, and everything seemed slipshod and off—not corrupt or bad, though.

"Not once did I feel like everything would work out simply because we loved each other, or that we could just relax and enjoy ourselves. It felt different."

"Like this room does right now?" I asked.

"Yes. You can't move. But there was something good between us, too, beautiful, like a meadow of flowers. That's why we stayed together. We both gave something positive to the relationship."

"I could tell that."

"It's really raining hard."

"Yeah, quite a downpour. And it's gotten kind of cold."

The languor of the night rain crept into the room. The rain beat down with a sad, lonely rhythm. Through the rain-streaked windowpanes, the streetlights looked a cool blue, and the room seemed to turn a deeper shade of black. I knew we shouldn't stay there any longer. It was difficult for me to move, but I knew that we would be in trouble if we didn't leave. My chest filled with the air of loneliness. This wasn't right.

"I'll take a taxi home. Will you help me find one?" I asked.

"Okay. I feel like I've been standing in the surf with big waves pounding down on me. I'm totally bushed. What a strange feeling."

"Let's get out of here. We've gotta go now," I said, on the verge of tears. I felt miserable. Something dark was pushing down on me so hard that I almost didn't want to live.

"Let's go," I repeated.

Otohiko stood up silently.

Before I got into the taxi, I asked, "Are you going back to her place?"

"No, I'm not."

I felt relieved. I couldn't leave him there by himself.

"I'll go look for her at the bar where she works, or at places where she usually hangs out."

"Do you want me to help?"

"You're in no shape to be doing anything. Maybe tomorrow when you're feeling better. I'll be in touch."

He closed the door. I waved, and watched him recede into the distance. I watched until he disappeared beyond the horizon and into the darkness, and was swallowed up by the rain.

I didn't know where Sui was, and neither she nor Otohiko called me. Several times, I dreamed that Sui had died. Every time I had the dream, I would wake up with a start, covered with sweat. Then I wouldn't be able to get back to sleep, and I'd get up and read the newspaper cover to cover. With trepidation, I'd watch the news on television. I didn't learn anything.

To my amazement, Sui started to recede into the distance after three or four days. I was surprised at the shallowness of my attachment, and also at my ability to separate myself from her, and from the others, and from the feelings I had had for them. Perhaps I had been released from the bonds that held me.

The whole summer seemed like something that had happened in a dream. It wasn't a bad dream, though. It was pleasant, like a day from childhood. I had done everything I could do in that dream. There was nothing more for me to accomplish, and so I decided to move on, and not dwell on it. It only upset me to think about it anyway.

On the fifth day, I heard from Saki. I was asleep when she

called, but I had become extremely quick about picking up the phone.

"Hello?"

"Hi. It's me, Saki."

"Good morning."

"What are you saying? It's past noon. Anyway, you'll never guess where I am—the airport!" she said excitedly. I could indeed hear those special sounds you hear only at the airport in the background, all the hustle-bustle and tension that makes your heart skip.

"Where are you headed?"

"To see a friend in New York. I also need to buy a bunch of books for a paper that I'm writing."

"But why so suddenly?" I asked.

"Ever since Sui disappeared, Otohiko has been moping around at home all the time. I couldn't take it anymore, and so I thought I'd get away."

"That's not a nice thing for a big sister to do to her baby brother."

"If that's what you think, why don't you go and see him?" Saki said with a laugh. "You know, I think that one period in our life has come to an end. Not just because Sui disappeared—it's not that simple. Something is really over. We don't have anything to hide anymore, but, to me, it's more of a relief than something I miss. I should take this occasion to celebrate and even have some fun, right? That's what most Japanese girls would do, huh? So I've decided to travel, and see the sights, and visit my old friends. I can't really explain it, but that's what I want to do. And you know what? My intuition tells me that Sui's still alive. She'll live, as long as she's not with Otohiko."

"I'm not so sure."

"I feel sure. It just doesn't feel like she's dead to me. And, Kazami, thanks for everything. You saved me."

"You'll be back soon, won't you?"

It felt like we were saying farewell.

"Oh sure, as soon as summer break's over. We can hang out on campus together again after I get back," Saki said.

She was an enigma to me, but she became my friend that summer, and was so sweet, and calm, and plucky. I'd always liked her.

"Okay, I'll see you in the fall."

"Bye."

"Take care."

I heard the click when she hung up the phone, and the airport scene vanished from my mind. For all I knew, she might never come back. Or was I just being paranoid? I would see her again in the fall. Saki is different from her. Yes, she is. The thought made me all choked up again.

★　★　★

Dear Kazami,

How are you? I'm fine. I'm four months pregnant now. Please don't worry about me. I have found a man who is willing to be a father to my baby, and he wants me to marry him. He's a miracle to me.

I wanted to let you know what is going on in my life. I had a number of choices available to me:

1. I could have an abortion and stay with Otohiko.
2. Have an abortion and break up with Otohiko.
3. Have an abortion and marry the man who wants me.
4. Keep the baby and marry the man.
5. Suicide.
6. Love suicide with Otohiko.

It would have been impossible to have the baby and stay with Otohiko. I was painfully aware of that. In fact, it hurt me so much that I nearly lost my mind. I felt the deepest despair. If I had followed the plot line set out for my life more faithfully, I may have been able to do it.

I waited for my period, but when I didn't get it again, I had no doubt about being pregnant. Then I came back to Japan and started living by myself. Low on money and energy, I had to face reality.

I feel certain that my life story, as I knew it, demanded that I die. My mother succumbed to despair. I believed that death was preferable to despair, because at least one does not have to harbor any hope.

I've wanted to die for a long time. I really, truly wanted to. You probably think it ridiculous that I had difficulty choosing between marriage, romance, and death, because they all seemed about the same to me.

Even when I was a little girl, I seriously thought that I could not avoid dying young. That conviction was my curse. I don't know about other people, but I imagine that something like that lurks inside everyone. In other words, everyone has their own private hell. I think that's what Father wrote about in his book—the type of man who will have sex with a girl young enough to be his daughter, if he can find a pretty young Japanese thing who is having a hard time living abroad. And then the girl turns out to be his daughter. And there's Otohiko, who is a pessimist even when he's in love, and Shoji, who had no hope at all for his life, even though he had a cute high school girl who adored him.

Of course, it's not as simple as all that. It's not a matter of good and evil. Traits like that have deep roots within a person, and sometimes they appear as talent, or a personality flaw. It circulates through your body just as your blood does and makes you the person you are. It's not fate, it's what you have inside. If that weren't the case,

Otohiko and I would still be in beautiful Boston. We would have been married in a lovely little chapel, and be living there as husband and wife. But that was a story, and it never happened. Partly because we are brother and sister, and partly because we chose to break up, as many couples do after treading the same path for a time.

I'm sorry for going on so long about my own personal problems, but I thought that you would want to know, and would understand. I wrote only a short note to Otohiko (that's a better way to leave your lover).

In any case, everything pointed to dying as the best possible choice for me, and that's what I decided to do. I had lost my confidence in my ability to stay alive. I was all choked up inside. I sat down and wrote out my options on a piece of paper, and considered them carefully. You know what I chose. I felt as though I've altered my own fate.

That's what I chose, but then I didn't have the strength to carry it out. I called you, but then it seemed too much trouble to talk things over with you. I considered a love suicide with you. I felt so isolated and out of it that I thought that it wouldn't be so lonely to die next to you, and so I wanted to give you just enough to knock you out. Then I put too much of the drug into your stew by mistake. I knew that it wouldn't kill you, but then I realized that I didn't have enough to kill myself. I had a friend who would give me more, so I decided to go over and get some while you were still asleep. I was in a hurry to die. It was at that moment that you sat up like a zombie, and it blew my mind. Your eyes were barely open, and your voice wild. You really scared me, but you also moved me. I know that sounds stupid, but I was truly moved. After I got out of the apartment, I stood outside the door crying, and then I went back in. You were sound asleep. Your face looked as peaceful as a death mask. I gathered together a few of my things, said good night to you, and then left that room forever. Don't worry. The rent is paid.

Soon, my name will be put on his family register as his wife. He was a customer at the bar where I worked, and he has savings, and is actually a very kind man. I'm not just saying that to save my pride. He's older, and actually I like his type much more than Otohiko.

I'm going to have the baby. My future husband's blood type is the same as Otohiko's so I don't think anyone will find out. Morning sickness is rough, but a kind of pain I prefer to being beaten by my mother. It will really upset me if the baby has three eyes, or only one leg, or six fingers on one of her hands, or something even worse. But

I'll deal with that if and when it happens. I'm ashamed to
write this, but one can always abort the fetus.

I've thought about you many times since we met. You
seem like a caretaker to me. It's been painful for me. I was
living in a bizarre little dream world of my own making,
and then you entered my life suddenly, and it felt like a
blow. Like on the day we first met when we went to the
park at noontime, and you bought me a Popsicle, and it
melted really quickly. Like when I was little and I was
doing something naughty at a friend's house, the image of
my mother's face would suddenly flash through my mind.
Like when I'm on a date with someone who I don't really
like, and then something reminds me of a guy I do like,
and I feel blue.

I always enjoyed being with you. You have a nice life
and a bright future. Sometimes I would be watching you,
your shortcomings, brightness, clumsiness, sweetness,
glumness, your gestures, and somehow I felt as if I might
be able to like myself a little better, and other people too.
It was the first time that I accepted the world outside me
as it is. It was a shock.

It wasn't only the way you looked, or times you and I

spent together. I began to perceive your colors in many things around me, and I started to feel that there might be some way out. I'd see these colors in the sun and the road, in cars, and flowers along the road, and in the windows of buildings.

Now, what reminds me of you most is the mailbox. You can find one anywhere, except for when you're really looking for one. There will be one in the most unexpected places, like lonely street corners. On clear days and rainy days, morning and night, everywhere in the world, just as the moon reflects in every lake, stream, and ocean.

I hated leaving on that rainy night. I felt just like a pony who'd been sold and had to leave its mother. I longed for the summer, when I could see you and Otohiko. As I rode away, I kept thinking of mailboxes so that I wouldn't be pulled back again. I focused on that completely.

The only path that connects me to you and Otohiko now is the mail. (I don't want to call on the phone, because I can't express myself and besides I'd feel wretched after I hung up.) Mailboxes stand for that connection between us, and here I am, writing you a letter to put in that box.

I will be a good mother to Otohiko's child. I will do my best. If all goes well, I may even live to see the day when she starts kindergarten, and when she attends the Adults' Day ceremony at age twenty-one. I want a baby girl. Saki will continue her research. Otohiko will at last regain his sanity.

I will think of you every time I see a mailbox. Life goes on. You and I will never meet again. Take care. I do want to see you again.

Sui

It was early September. After staying up all night trying to finish a rush translation project, I fell asleep at dawn. When I woke up, it was already past noon. I had a craving for a Coke, so I went down to a vending machine to buy a can. After that, I went out for a walk. When I got home, I peeked into my mail slot for the first time in a while, and saw her letter. I got myself a beer, curled up on my bed, and read it. It was a good letter.

For a while after I finished it, I closed my eyes and lay there, the letter still in my hand. The sunlight that filtered in through the curtain looked red through my eyelids, and I felt like I was on the summer beach, a warm breeze blowing over my face as I sat listening to the waves break. I felt sleepy again. It was my own little bit of summer.

When I woke up, it was already evening and the sunlight shone a bright gold. The color of the sky right before sunset was exactly the same as it is at dawn, but then, in reverse of the morning, the sky grows darker and darker.

Released from all the stress that had built up within me, I

174

felt empty. It was a pleasant emptiness. I realized that I had to make my next move. That I knew for sure. I decided to take a trip, although not as long a trip as Saki's. I no longer had to wait for bad omens, or for Sui's unexpected visits. And I'd wanted to go to the beach that summer anyway.

I took the rest of the day and packed carefully. I had considered burying the little wooden box somewhere, but I put it into my suitcase instead. If Sui had died, the black knit skirt would have been my memento of her. I could have become a collector of mementos, but I was spared that distinction. I remembered my white slacks still hanging on the line on her porch. I felt both sad and strange. In a matter of months, they would probably be packed away with the rest of Sui's things.

When I put the chip of Shoji's bone in the bag, I could hear it clink against the side of the box. The sound echoed in my ears for a moment, just as the rhythm of the surf stays with you. I remembered nestling up against his shoulder when we went for a drive, and finding just the right place for my head to rest, without getting in the way of his driving. It wasn't his face that remained in my mind, but his shoulder, and hands gripping the steering wheel. Now all that was left of him was tucked in my bag, an object that once was a living person. I was glad that Sui hadn't died.

I took a shower and left the house before my hair had dried. The late afternoon sun, filled with the scent of evening, washed over the street with clear light. From in front of the houses on either side of the road, the trees cast their pale shadows on the pavement.

Suddenly, I remembered my first visit to Saki's apartment. It seemed like a long time ago, when life was still peaceful. Then it occurred to me that I should stop in and see Otohiko on my way out of town. I felt sorry for him, all alone in that house. He probably had gotten a letter from Sui, too, although his was undoubtedly much more abrupt and to the point. In my haste to leave for the beach, I had nearly forgotten about him. I almost wished that I had brought the letter from Sui with me, but then I owed it to Sui to keep that to myself.

I finally reached his place. I rang the doorbell and Otohiko answered right away.

"Hello."

"Come on in."

When I saw his face, I suddenly felt overcome with warmth and happiness. I wondered whether that was how men felt when they encounter old war buddies. And then my heart filled both with the satisfaction of our having accomplished something together, though we'd known each other only briefly, and the bitterness of having lost something else forever. The day had been so intense, and I was sad about the summer coming to an end, as though I were an eighteen-year-old again. I nodded and went in.

"Saki's not here. She went on a trip," he said, and poured me a cup of coffee.

"I know. She called me."

I noticed that Saki's part of the apartment had been cleaned out, and I started to feel uneasy again.

"I heard from Sui. Did you?"

I nodded.

"I'm happy that she's alive. I really am," he said, but he looked down.

"I'm glad, too."

I wondered how much she had told him in her letter. I was too scared to say anything about it. Maybe she'd lied to him; maybe she hadn't. In any case, she'd made her decision and there was nothing he could do about it, except perhaps to find her and make yet another attempt at a relationship. Then someone would have died for sure. I knew that he had decided against that course of action and guessed that was why he looked so grim now.

A lukewarm breeze blew in through the open door, mixing with the cold air coming out of the air-conditioner.

"What's that big bag?" he asked somberly.

"I'm just going on a short trip."

"*Et tu, Brutus*. Where are you going? Are you traveling alone?"

For some reason, I felt kind of guilty.

"Yeah."

"How long will you be gone?

"I haven't decided yet."

"I'll do the driving. I'll take you anywhere you want. Let me go with you."

I scowled at him. He explained, "All of a sudden, I feel jealous. I promise that I'll behave myself—I'm too exhausted for that sort of thing anyway. I just don't want to be in this house, can you understand that? I feel like being with other people. Besides, it's always nice to have another person along when you're on a trip."

I thought about what he had said. I wanted to tell him to go by himself, but I couldn't. It was just like him to propose something like this.

"Okay, but only for one day. Tomorrow, we'll split up and go our separate ways," I said.

"Fine. I'll go see a friend in Yokohama tomorrow."

"I was meaning to go down that way, too, so that will work out well."

"All I want is a reason to get out of here. It seemed like so much trouble but now that I can leave with you . . . I appreciate it."

He smiled for the first time since I arrived.

I went out and got a rental car while I was waiting for him to finish packing.

"Let's buy some food and have a picnic on the beach."

"Sounds good. And we can build a bonfire too."

I felt happier than I had for a long time.

We got on the highway and headed toward the beach. I took it all in—the vibration of the car, the sound of the warning bell that rang when we went over the speed limit, the buildings receding into the distance, and the high clear night sky. There was a pale half-moon and Venus was shining bright. I sensed that everything that had recently transpired existed in the dusk sky as it turned into night, over the land to the ocean. These things happen sometimes. All the beauty in what I had witnessed—from the shallow to the intense—filled my heart, and it moved from a position deep within my soul up high into the sky, the vast ceiling that revolved above us. It became part of the scene before me.

* * *

Otohiko said, "I wonder if she'll ever come back."

"I really don't think so," I said.

"It feels strange to me, like my body's gotten lighter. Like I'm about to lose myself."

"How many years ago did you meet her?"

"Six, maybe more. I needed a break after all those years. I can't even remember what we were doing all that time," he said, his eyes on the road.

"Did you look for her any more?"

"I searched for her every day, like a detective. I haven't gotten much sleep lately. It hurt me so much when I read that letter that I cried."

"You thought that she was dead?"

"I was overcome with despair, and I was so down myself, that I thought she might have killed herself. I searched for her during the day and stayed at her place at night. Every hour, I'd check my answering machine at home."

"You did all that?"

"Yes. She sounded just fine in the letter, but she must be hurting too. I'm so glad she survived. I think that she chose what was best for her."

"I'm glad that you feel that way," I said.

"But if you hadn't shown up today, I might have killed myself tonight. Not really, but that letter was a huge letdown."

For a brief moment, it occurred to me that he just might have done it.

"This is the first time in a long time I've made a bonfire on the beach," Otohiko said as he gathered driftwood. We unpacked all the things that we had bought at the store—fireworks, wine, fried chicken. It was so dark that I couldn't see him if he moved even a few feet away from me. I watched the waves and enjoyed the sensation of the ocean air blowing over me. The sea was a hundred times vaster than I had imagined, and I felt as though I would be swallowed up. The waves kept pounding down on the shore, and Venus and the moon lingered in the sky.

"I bet that you were a Boy Scout."

"How do you know?"

It was the way he neatly stacked the wood for the fire.

"I don't know. You're that type."

"Well, excuse me. I have lived on the beach before, you know."

"When was that?"

Otohiko usually seemed flat and annoyed at having to talk about anything, but this trip to the beach had relaxed him. Even when we were on our way there in the car, I could sense the gloom within him. We weren't talking, but I could tell that he was overcome with emotion. I could understand what hurt him, but I could do nothing to relieve him of the weight of time. The image of him getting up to go and see Sui at dusk popped into my mind. I considered the deep scars that he bore from spending countless days convinced that he should continue living that way forever. He looked at loose ends.

"It wasn't long after Father died, and Mom wasn't feeling well. We went to the beach so that she could recuperate. We would often set off fireworks and make bonfires. We had lots of friends on the beach, and they taught us all the tricks of the trade."

"Did you have fun?"

"I don't really remember. For some reason, living on the beach didn't feel real to me."

"Aren't bonfires supposed to be bigger and brighter than this?"

We finally got the wood to light, but the fire remained small. It could barely compete with the powerful darkness of the beach.

"It just takes a little time! Be patient."

His face looked bright in the faint light of the fire. I thought of the conversation with my mother about losing yourself in something. Otohiko sat there on the sand, tossing one branch after another into the flames. Is this what she meant?

"How about some wine?"

Just as I had with Sui that night, I poured some wine for him, only this time into a plastic cup.

He took a sip and said, "Nice wine. It might cool down a lot out here at night."

"It's fall already."

"Yeah, I guess that's why we built the bonfire first, instead of doing the fireworks."

"Let's do the fireworks later, okay?"

"Do you think we can warm up the chicken over the fire?"

"I brought some skewers so we could."

"You're good."

"And then we can wrap the biscuits in foil and stick them on the fire for just a minute."

"You've thought of everything."

"You're supposed to be the outdoor expert. Where's your mess kit, anyway?"

I got a buzz from the wine, and I kept wondering why, all of a sudden, I found myself there on the beach with him. In fact, I had grown used to that sort of thing happening to me.

The thunderous waves were the only novelty. The whitecaps of the surf; the strong scent of salt water; the rough feel of the sand; the horizon silently breathing in the distance; the sparkling lights of the town; headlights floating by like satellites in the sky as cars moved slowly down the coast.

The fire burned more brightly as the sky grew darker and darker. Sparks flew out onto the beach, illuminating the white sand. It wasn't a roaring fire, but it crackled loud enough to cover the sound of the surf and stave off the darkness.

"I love watching the flames."

"Me too."

The surface of the ocean shimmered, and it looked like a big piece of black cloth gently undulating on a stage. I pulled out the small wooden box from my bag and tossed it into the fire. It burst into flames and flared up brightly. I was afraid it might give off a strange smell, but it was undetectable in the sea air. This was much better than a crematorium. I believed that.

"You are very solemn."

I asked if he knew what I had just thrown into the fire.

"A chip of bone?" he said, not looking my way. I turned toward the fire and pressed my palms together.

"You've heard everything, haven't you?"

"She would tell me absolutely everything, scary things and

trivial things. So I knew. She held back in that letter to me, though."

"Oh yeah?"

She dumped him. They broke up with each other. Whatever—the fact remained that they weren't together anymore. It was all over. The promise that each had made to themselves in their hearts resounded like waves breaking again and again.

"I'm embarrassed to admit it, but I brought something too."

He pulled out a bundle of onionskin paper from his bag. "What's that?"

"My father's ninety-ninth story."

He peeled off one page at a time and threw them into the fire. Each sheet danced up in the air as it burned and turned into black ash.

"Did your father give you that?"

"Yes, he sent it to me just before he died. I showed it to Mom, but she said that I should have it."

"What about the copy that Sui had?"

"The one she sent to Saki? That was the same thing, only in Sui's handwriting. I think she probably copied it when he was asleep."

"You're kidding."

I remembered what Sui was going through that day.

"I never told you?"

"So you mean that you never told Sui you had the original?"

"How could I?"

"Did you tell Saki?"

"No. I didn't care if Sui showed it to her, but I thought that she would be really upset if she learned that other people had copies, and that those other people were me and Saki. That was the only thing she had of Father's."

"Really? And you knew that?"

I imagined Sui, still a young teenage girl, copying her father's manuscript in the dark. The pages had burned into brittle black hollow balls, and the wind blew them down the beach toward the sea.

"Since we're on the subject, I wanted to tell you something about the last section of the ninety-eighth story, the part you praised. I wrote that."

"What?"

I sat there silently for a while.

"He left the ninety-eighth story at our house, and it was unfinished. When I first met Sui, she told me that she wanted very much to read the story, and so I took it to her secretly. Even though the story was about Sui, for some reason there was no ending. I thought that it would hurt her to read the story just as he had left it, plus I knew that she had the ninety-ninth story.

"Sui knew that her mother would never come back to her, and she came to Japan to stay with relatives, but it wasn't working out. I just added that ending to the story, and gave it to her, and then she went and took it to Shoji. Only the ninety-eighth story, though."

I didn't say anything.

"It's all in the past now," he said. "Should we warm up the chicken? I feel a little strange about doing that after you put that bone in there."

"Human beings are flesh, too."

"I guess you're right." He smiled.

"What a relief."

"For me, too."

"I feel like I've rid myself of a phantom."

"I do too. Plus, I'm happy to be here. I'd been wanting to go to the beach for a long time," I said, and nibbled on some chicken.

Otohiko pulled the biscuits out of the flames, and said, "I'm really enjoying talking with you. I think I'm kinda drunk."

He opened the foil packet. It smelled delicious.

"Uh-oh. They got a little burnt."

Otohiko smiled, and said, "Maybe it's also because I haven't been talking to other people much these days."

"Maybe it's because of the fire."

"Maybe because of this breeze."

"Like they say, the ocean makes people open their hearts and minds."

"I enjoy it even when we're doing small talk."

"No matter what we talk about, the waves just keep breaking off in the distance."

"It's liberating, somehow."

"I agree. This wine isn't cold, but it tastes good."

"Shall I put it in the cooler?"

"There's one in there already."

"I'm glad I came. I'm having a good time. It was good of you."

"My pleasure. I wouldn't really want to be doing this by myself."

I nibbled on my biscuit.

"The moon is so white."

"Yes, it looks very small."

"I think there are probably lots of stars out, too, but the fire's giving off so much light that we can't see them."

"You're probably right. Maybe we could have even seen the Milky Way."

I waved my arm in the air to indicate the path of the big river of stars that cuts across the sky.

"There's a white bird in the center of it."

"No one else is around."

"Yeah, it's quiet."

I turned around and saw the tall hotels surrounding the beach in this resort town.

"Do you think that they can see our fire from way up in those hotels?"

"Where shall we stay tonight?"

"One of these places has got to have vacancies."

"There are rooms without any lights on, so they must have some empty rooms."

"Or the people in them could be asleep, or out."

"I'm sure we'll find something. It's a weekday after all."

"I like that one with bay windows. It's really neat the way it's built."

"That's the way the summer homes are around here."

"It doesn't even seem like we're in Japan."

"Do you have any money?"

"Credit cards."

"I brought a bunch too."

"If we're going to travel more, we should be thrifty."

He laughed. I felt like we would just keep right on traveling.

"Let's have a drink at the hotel bar."

"That sounds good. I could use some hot sake."

I felt as though I could clearly hear the sound of the waves wrapping the silence into themselves as the night grew late.

The broad, open scene before me took away all my gloom, and the fresh air filled my heart. A certain light, though, kept on shining and wouldn't ever go out. All was calm. It was an eternal pure night like at the world's end.

I had imagined that it was a night like this in the last scene of the ninety-eighth story. The sad, fatalistic song of the mermaid heard only faintly. Her tail covered with scales, which could not be touched. The sad profile. The moonlight. "I shall love my beautiful one always."

"You actually wrote that part of the story?"

"Don't remind me of it."

"I always wondered why the style changes suddenly there, you know."

"Enough."

"Was it Saki? Sui?"

"Everyone, both of them."

"We'll never see Sui again. Post boxes—what the hell?"

"Are you crying?"

I was crying a little. If we hadn't been on the beach, the absence would have struck me more forcefully. We had spent that summer together just so that we could part. He was the one friend I had left of the three. I'd never see her again. I'd never get an afternoon phone call from her again.

"You'd better quit crying, or you're going to make me cry, too."

190

"I've stopped already."

"Good girl," Otohiko said, looking forlorn and for all the world like he was about to cry. "Do you want me to go to bed with you?"

"Hey, that was supposed to be my line."

"I think I'm falling in love with you."

"Shut up."

"I'll think about it again in autumn."

"Fine," I said.

"That's what I'll do."

I looked at Otohiko. I saw the sky and sea and sand and the flickering flames of the bonfire through my tears. All at once, it rushed into my head at tremendous speed, and made me feel dizzy. It was beautiful. Everything that had happened was shockingly beautiful, enough to make you crazy.

AFTERWORD

The director Alexandro Jodorowsky once said about his film *El Topo*, "If you're great, *El Topo* is a great picture. If you're limited, *El Topo* is limited." These words inspired me in my creation of the character Sui in *N.P.* That is, some readers will regard Sui as a fallen woman, while others will see her as a boddhisattva, a being who defers her own salvation in order to help others attain theirs. I don't feel confident about my portrayal of Sui, but I do hope to have improved on some shortcomings found in my other books.

Spatially, *N.P.* takes place in a very small world, and it involves only a limited number of characters, but I have attempted, in this miniature universe, to touch on as many of the themes that interest me as possible (lesbianism, love within the family, telepathy and empathy, the occult, religion, and so on).

The eighteen months during which I worked on *N.P.* were both challenging and interesting. I constantly had doubts about my approach, but at the same time I reminded myself that a degree of self-searching and doubt are healthy for any project. You have to start somewhere.

I'm sure that you have encountered troubled people in your life, as I have. Whether brilliant or ordinary, they have to cope with some burden that constantly makes their lives difficult. When I was writing *N.P.*, I had such people in mind. I wanted to communicate the notion that such people should be able to live as they please, without interference from others. Anyone should, for that matter.

I would like to express deep thanks to Chiaki Nakanishi and Ryoichi Takayanagi of Kadokawa Shoten who waited patiently for this book. I appreciated Masayasu Ishihara's encouragement, as well. I have benefited greatly from discussions with Mizuho Ozawa, a translator who kindly advised me on the craft of translation.

I also wish to thank Masumi Hara, one of contemporary Japan's top artists, for the fantastic cover illustration of the Japanese edition, as well as the book's designer, Masahiro Yamaguchi.

I also appreciate the many letters of encouragement from my readers. I am most grateful that you have taken the time to read *N.P.*

> *On a sunny November afternoon,*
> *with a cold, eating a persimmon*

BANANA YOSHIMOTO